In the Fifth at

This is the
in the Malory Towers series

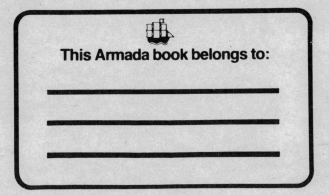

This Armada book belongs to:

_____

_____

_____

Enid Blyton

In the Fifth at Malory Towers

ARMADA

First published in the UK in 1950
by Methuen & Co. Ltd
Republished by Dragon Books in 1967
First published in Armada in 1988
This impression 1990

Armada is an imprint of
the Children's Division, part of
the Harper Collins Publishing Group,
8 Grafton Street, London W1X 3LA

Printed and bound in Great Britain by
William Collins Sons & Co. Ltd, Glasgow

"Felicity! Look – there's Malory Towers at last!" cried Darrell. "I always look out for it at this bend. This is where we catch a glimpse of it first."

Felicity gazed at the big square-looking building of grey stone standing high up on a cliff by the sea. At each end was a rounded tower.

"North Tower, East Tower, South Tower, West Tower," said Felicity. "I'm glad we're in North Tower, overlooking the sea. Are you glad to be going back, Darrell?"

"Yes, awfully. Are you?" asked her sister, still with her eyes glued to the gracious building in the distance.

"Yes, I am really. But I do hate saying goodbye to Mother and Daddy, and Cook and Jane and the dogs and the cat, and . . . "

"The robin in the garden and the six hens and the ducks and the goldfish and the earwigs on the verandah!" finished Darrell, with a laugh. "Don't be such a goose, Felicity. You know quite well that as soon as you set foot in the grounds of Malory Towers you'll love being there!"

"Oh yes, I know I shall," said Felicity. "But it's quite a different world from the world of Home. And it's a bit difficult suddenly going from one to the other."

"Well, all I can say is – we're lucky to have two such marvellous worlds to live in!" said Darrell. "Home – and Malory Towers! Look, who's that in that car?"

Felicity leaned out to see. "It's June," she said. "June – and Alicia her cousin."

Darrell snorted. She didn't like the first-former June. "Don't you go and get friendly with that sly, brazen little June again," she warned Felicity. "You know what happened last term. You stick to Susan."

"I'm going to," said Felicity. "You needn't tell me things like that. I'm not a new girl now. I'm in my second term."

"Wish I was!" said Darrell. "I hate to think that every term the day I leave comes nearer."

"Well, it's the same for me," said Felicity. "Only I don't bother about it yet with so many terms in front of me. I say – fancy you being a fifth-former this term! In the Fifth at Malory Towers – gosh, it does sound grand. And me only a first-former."

"Yes. You first-formers do seem babies to me now," said Darrell. "Absolute kids! It's funny to think how I looked up to the fifth-formers when I was in the first, and hardly dared to speak to one; and if one spoke to me I almost fell through the ground. I don't notice anything like that about *you*, young Felicity!"

"Oh well – I suppose it's because you're my sister," said Felicity. "I'm not falling through the ground just because you address a few words to me – no, not even if you are made head girl of the fifth!"

"Well, I shan't be," said Darrell. "I had my share of responsibility last term when I was head of the Upper Fourth. Anyway, I'd like to sit back and take a bit of a rest from responsibility this term. Last term was pretty hectic, what with being head girl, and having to go in for School Certificate, too!"

"But thank goodness you passed!" said Felicity, proudly. "And with all those credits, too! Did everyone in the Upper Fourth pass, do you know?"

"Not Gwen. Nor Alicia," said Darrell. "You remember she got measles during the exam? And Connie, Ruth's twin, didn't pass either. She'll be left down in the fourth, thank goodness. Now Ruth will be able to say a few words on her own!"

Connie and Ruth had both been in the Upper Fourth the term before, and the girls had often felt cross because Connie never gave Ruth a chance to speak for herself, but always answered for her. She looked after Ruth as if she were a baby sister, not a girl of her own age, nearly sixteen! Now, with Connie in a form below, Ruth would have a chance of being herself instead of Connie's shadow. That should be interesting.

"Here we are – sweeping into the drive!" said Felicity. "Mother – do look at Malory Towers. Isn't it super?"

Her mother turned round from the front seat of the car and smiled at the two enthusiastic faces behind her.

"Quite super, as you call it," she said.

"In fact, smashing!" said Mr Rivers, who was at the wheel. "Isn't that the right word, too, Felicity? It's the word I seem to have heard you use more than any other these holidays."

The girls laughed. "The lower school call everything smashing or smash," said Darrell, in rather a superior voice.

"And the upper school are too la-di-da for words!" began Felicity, eager to retaliate. But nobody heard because Mr Rivers came to a stop near the great flight of steps, and immediately they were all swamped in crowds of excited girls running here and there from cars and coaches. The train girls had just arrived in the coaches that brought them from the station, and there was such a tremendous noise of yelling and shouting and hooting of car horns that it was impossible to hear what anyone said.

"DARRELL!" screamed somebody, putting an excited face in at the window. "Good! I hoped you wouldn't be late. Sally's here somewhere."

The face disappeared, and another one came. "FELICITY! I thought it was you. Come on out!"

"Susan! I'm just coming!" shouted Felicity, and leapt out so suddenly that she fell over a pile of lacrosse sticks and almost knocked over a tall girl standing nearby saying goodbye to her parents.

"Felicity Rivers! Look where you're going," said a wrathful voice, and Felicity blushed and almost fell through the ground. It was Irene speaking, Irene who was now a fifth-former. Darrell grinned to herself. Aha! Felicity might cheek one fifth-former, her own sister – but she was still in awe of the big girls after all!

"Sorry, Irene," said Felicity in a meek voice. "Frightfully sorry."

Darrell jumped out too and was immediately surrounded by her friends.

"Darrell! I'll help you in with your things!"

"Hallo, Darrell, did you have good hols? I say, you passed your School Cert. jolly well. Congratulations!"

"Darrell Rivers! You never answered my letter last hols! And I wrote you pages!"

Darrell grinned round at the laughing faces. "Hallo, Alicia! Hallo, Sally! Irene, you nearly made my parents fall out of the car when you screamed in at the window just now. Hallo, Belinda! Done any good sketching in the hols?"

Mrs Rivers called out of the car, "Darrell! We shall be going in a few minutes, dear. Tell Sally to come and have a word with me."

Sally was Darrell's best friend, and her mother was a great friend of Mrs Rivers. She came up to the car and Mrs Rivers looked at her with approval. Sally

had once been such a prim, plain little first-former –
now she had blossomed out into a pretty, bonny girl,
sturdy and dependable, with very nice manners.

Mrs Rivers had a few words with her and then
looked round for Darrell, who was still talking away
to a crowd of her friends. Felicity was nowhere to be
seen.

"We must go now," she said to Sally. "Just tell
Darrell and Felicity, will you?"

"Darrell! You're wanted!" shouted Sally, and
Darrell turned and ran to the car. She was already
half lost in the world of Malory Towers.

"Oh, Mother – are you going? Thanks for most
lovely hols. Where's Felicity?"

Felicity was not to be found. So thrilled was she
at being back and hearing the excited voices of her
friends that she had gone off with them without
another thought! Darrell went to look for her.

"Anyone seen Felicity?"

Plenty of people had but nobody knew where she
was. "Blow her! She's gone up to her dormy, I suppose, to see what bed she's got this term," thought
Darrell and sped up to find her. But she wasn't there.
Darrell went down again and out to the car.

"I can't find her anywhere, Mother," she said.
"Can you wait a bit?"

"No, we can't," said Mr Rivers, impatiently. "I've
got to get back. Tell Felicity we wanted to say goodbye. We must go."

He gave Darrell a hug and then she hugged her
mother, too. Mr Rivers put in the clutch and the car
moved slowly off.

There was a shriek behind him. "Daddy! Don't
go without saying goodbye. You were!"

"I was," said her father, with a grin exactly like
Darrell's. "Can't wait about for girls who forget their

mother and father a quarter of a minute after arriving."

"I didn't forget you, of course I didn't," protested Felicity, still hanging on the running board. "I just wanted to go and see our form room. It's all been done up in the hols and looks super. Goodbye, Daddy." She gave him a bear hug that almost knocked off his hat.

She ran round to the other side and gave her mother a hug, too. "I'll write on Sunday. Give my love to Cook and Jane and the gardener, and the dogs, and . . . "

The car was moving! "Jump off unless you want to come back home again!" called her father. "If you do, get in the back!"

But she didn't want to! She jumped off, laughing. She and Darrell stood waving as the car made its way slowly down the crowded drive. Then it moved out of the gate with other cars, and was gone.

Felicity turned to Darrell with shining eyes. "Isn't it fun to be back again? Did you feel like that your second term, Darrell? I'm not nervous or shy any more as I was last term. I belong now. I know everyone. It's smashing!"

She tore up the steps at top speed and collided with Mam'zelle Dupont.

"*Tiens!* Another mad girl! Felicity, I will not have you . . . "

But Felicity was gone. Mam'zelle's face broke into a smile as she gazed after her. "These girls! Anyone would think they were glad to be back."

More Arrivals

The first day of term and the last day were always exciting. Nobody bothered about rules and regulations, everyone talked at the tops of their voices, and as for *walking* down the corridors or up the stairs, well it just wasn't done, except by the staid sixth-formers and the mistresses.

It was fun to go and see what bed you had in the dormy, and whose bed was next to yours. It was fun to go and peep into your classroom and see if it looked any different. It was fun to say "how do you do" to all the mistresses, and especially to tease Mam'zelle Dupont. Not Mam'zelle Rougier, though, the other French mistress. She was as sharp as Mam'zelle Dupont was simple, and as irritable as the other was good tempered. Nobody ever teased Mam'zelle Rougier.

Darrell went to look for the rest of her friends in the fifth form. Fifth form! How grand it sounded! She was actually in the fifth now, with only one more form to go into. Oh dear – she was certainly getting very grown up.

Alicia and Sally came up, with Irene and Belinda. "Let's go and see our new classroom," said Darrell. "The fifth! My goodness!"

They all went along together. The new classroom was an extremely nice one, high up and overlooking the cliff. Down below was the blue Cornish sea, as blue as cornflowers today, the waves tipped with snowy white.

11

"I say – this is a wizard room, isn't it?" said Alicia, looking round. "Lovely windows and view – nice pictures – and all done up in cream and green."

"Any new girls, does anyone know?" asked Darrell, leaning out of the window and sniffing the salty sea air.

"There's someone called Maureen coming," said Irene. "I heard about her. The school she was at shut down suddenly, when the head died – and she's coming here. I don't know anything about her, though."

"I suppose *you're* coming into the fifth, Alicia?" said Sally. "I mean – I know Connie's been left down in the fourth because she didn't pass her School Cert. – and you didn't either, because you had the measles. But surely you won't be left down?"

"Oh no. I'm up all right!" said Alicia. "Gosh, I wouldn't have come back if I hadn't been put up with the rest of you. Miss Grayling wrote to Mother and said I could pass School Cert. on my head any time I liked and I could go up into the fifth with you, and work for School Cert. on the side, so to speak."

"Anyone left down with us from the old fifth form?" asked Darrell.

"Yes – Catherine Gray and Moira Linton," said Irene, promptly. There were groans from the others.

"Oh I *say* – two of the worst of them!" said Sally. "I never did like Moira – hard, domineering creature! Why has she been left down?"

"Well, actually she's a year young for the sixth," said Irene, "so they said she'd better stay down a year – but personally I think she was so unpopular that they just dropped her thankfully and went on without her!"

"What about Catherine?" asked Sally.

"She hasn't been well," said Irene. "Worked herself too hard, or something. She's pretty pious, isn't she? I don't really know much about her. She's one

12

of those girls that don't make much impression from a distance."

"Well, as far as we're concerned that's like three new girls then," said Darrell. "Catherine, Moira and Maureen. Who'll be head girl?"

"You or Sally," said Irene, promptly.

"No. I don't think so," said Darrell. "I imagine it will have to be either Catherine or Moira – after all, they've been fifth-formers for ages. It wouldn't be fair to put an ex-fourth-former over them at once."

"No. You're right," said Alicia. "Gosh, I hope it isn't Moira then. She does love to get her own way! Did you hear how she set all the second-formers a long poem to learn last term, to say at Monitors' Meeting, just because one of them wrote a poem about her, and nobody would own up to it? Every single one of them had to learn 'Kubla Khan'. They did howl about it!"

"Yes. I remember now," said Darrell. "Oh well, I dare say we shall manage Moira all right."

"If you lose your temper with her often enough!" said Irene, with a sly grin. Darrell's hot temper was well known. She had tried to conquer it for terms and terms, and just when she prided herself on really having got the better of it at last, out it came again.

Darrell looked ruefully at the others. "Yes. I'll have to be careful. I lost it really well last term, didn't I, Alicia, with that brazen young cousin of yours, June. I hope she behaves better this term!"

"She came to stay with us in the hols," said Alicia. "I've got three brothers, you know – and when June actually dared to disobey Sam, he gave her the choice of being spanked twenty times with her own hairbrush or running round our paddock twenty times each day!"

"And which did she choose?" asked everyone.

"Oh, running round the paddock, of course," said Alicia. "And Mother was awfully surprised to see her going round and round it each day like that. She thought she was training for sports or something! Sam stood and watched her, grinning like anything. So she *may* be better this term!"

"She can do with a lot of improvement!" said Darrell. "I say – what in the world's that?"

It was the sound of thunderous hooves out in the drive somewhere – so thunderous that the noise even came round to the back of Malory Towers and was heard in the classroom where the five girls stood listening.

"*I* know! It's old Bill back – and her brothers have brought her as usual – all on horseback!" cried Belinda, rushing out of the room. "Come along – let's go into the art room and look out of the window. We can see the drive from there."

They were soon leaning out of the high window. They saw a sight which they had already seen two or three times before, and were never tired of!

Wilhelmina, called Bill for short, had arrived on her horse, Thunder – and accompanying her were six of her seven brothers, all on horseback, too. What a sight they were, six well-grown boys, ranging from seventeen down to ten, with Bill, their sister, in the midst.

"Whoa there! Now then, quiet, quiet!"

"Thunder! We're here!"

"Bill, here's your case."

Clippity-clop, clippity-clop went the hooves of the seven grand horses, curvetting about the broad drive. "Hrrrrrrrmph!" said one of them, and then all seven neighed together.

"Bill, where can we let the horses drink?" came the deep voice of the seventeen-year-old brother.

14

"Follow me," said Bill, and the six brothers trotted up the drive and round a corner, following the girl sitting so straight on her magnificent horse, Thunder.

"Gosh!" said Alicia. "What a horde of brothers. Where's the seventh?"

"Gone into the army," said Sally. "My word – I wish *I* had seven brothers."

"Well, I've got three and that's more than enough," said Alicia. "No wonder Bill's more like a boy than a girl."

"Here they come again," said Irene. "Belinda, where's your sketchbook – do draw them all!"

Belinda had already got out her sketchbook which was always somewhere about her person. Her swift pencil sketched in horse after horse, and the others watched in admiration. Oh, to have a gift like Belinda's! She could draw anyone and anything.

The seven horses seemed to know that Bill and Thunder were to be left behind. They lifted their heads and whinnied softly. Bill leaned over and stroked the noses of those nearest to her.

"Goodbye, Moonlight. Goodbye, Starlight. Goodbye, Snorter. Goodbye, Sultan . . . "

"She's paying a lot more attention to the horses than to her brothers!" said Alicia, with a grin. "That's Bill all over, of course – horse-mad!"

"Well, her brothers are as bad!" said Sally. "Look – yelling goodbye to Thunder but not to Bill!"

"Off they go," said Darrell, envying Bill her brothers. "Look at Thunder, trying to follow them. He doesn't want to be left behind!"

Bill was left alone in the drive with the impatient Thunder, who thought he should go with his comrades; he reared and curvetted in annoyance at being made to go the other way, up the drive instead of down.

The six horses and brothers disappeared in a clatter of hooves and a cloud of dust. Bill, looking rather solemn, made Thunder take the path to the stables. She hated being parted from the many horses that her family owned. But now that she had settled down well at Malory Towers, and was allowed to bring her horse, she would not have given up boarding school for anything.

Another clatter of hooves, this time coming *up* the drive, made Bill rein in her horse, and look round. The five up in the art room yelled to her.

"Bill! BILL! Here comes Clarissa – and she's on her horse, too!"

Sure enough, up the drive came a beautiful little horse with white socks, tossing its pretty head and showing off. Clarissa Carter rode him. She had been a new girl the term before, a plain, bespectacled little thing with an ugly wire round her front teeth. But now she had no wire and no spectacles, and she galloped up, her auburn hair flying in the wind, and her green eyes shining.

"Bill! Bill! I've brought Merrylegs! Isn't he sweet? Oh, do let him see Thunder. They'll love one another."

"Two horse-mad creatures," said Alicia, with a laugh. "Well, Bill never had a friend till Clarissa came – so they'll have a fine time together this term, talking about horses and riding them, feeding them and grooming them . . . "

"Scrubbing their hooves and brushing their tails!" said Irene. "Gosh, those galloping hooves have given me an idea for a new tune – a galloping tune – like this!"

She hummed a galloping, lilting melody – "tirretty-tirretty-tirretty-too . . . "

"Dear old Irene – she's not horse-mad, she's music

16

mad," said Belinda, putting away her sketchbook. "Now we shall have nothing but galloping tunes for the next few weeks! Come on, tirretty-too!"

And she galloped her friend out of the room at top speed. "Tirretty-tirretty-tirretty-too. Oh – *so* sorry, Miss Potts – we never saw you coming!"

Supper time

All but the new girls were well settled in by the evening. Matron had received health certificates and pocket money from the lower school, and health certificates but no money from the upper school, who were allowed to keep their own without having to ask Matron for it.

"Did Irene's health certificate arrive all right?" asked Darrell, remembering how almost every term Irene's certificate was mislaid.

Sally laughed. "Oh, somebody put an envelope in Irene's case, marked 'Health Certificate', and she thought her mother had put it there instead of sending it by post – so she took it to Matron, of course, and said, 'Here you are, Matron – I've really remembered it at last!' "

"And what was inside it?" asked Darrell.

"A recipe for Bad Memories," chuckled Sally. "I forget how it went. Take a cupful of Reminders, and a spoonful of Scoldings – something like that. You should have seen Matron's face when she saw it. Irene was dumbfounded, of course. She would be! However, it didn't matter because Matron had got her certificate by post."

"Irene's such a scatterbrain, for all her cleverness," said Alicia. "So is Belinda. There must be something about art and music that makes people with those gifts perfectly idiotic over ordinary things. If Irene *can* lose something, she does. And if Belinda *can* forget something she forgets it! Do you remember how she came down to breakfast once without her blouse on?"

"There's the gong for supper," said Darrell, thankfully. "I'm awfully hungry. Hope there's as super a supper as usual – we always have such a good one on the first night! I'm glad I haven't got to fuss round Felicity this term – she's not a new girl any more. She can stand on her own feet."

They went down into the big dining room to supper. Sally absent-mindedly walked towards the fourth-form table, and Darrell pulled her back.

"Idiot! Do you want to sit with those kids?" she hissed. "*Here's* the fifth-form table!"

They took their places, and saw three girls already there, two old fifth-formers, and one new girl. Catherine and Moira nodded to them, and Catherine gave them a beaming smile. Moira didn't. She was tight-lipped and looked as if the cares of the whole school rested on her shoulders!

The new girl, Maureen, smiled at them brightly. She was a fluffy, rather untidy-looking girl, with a big mouth, a large nose and rather uneven teeth that stuck out a little and made her look rabbity.

"I'm Maureen Little," she said, in a light, friendly voice. "I hope you won't mind me at Malory Towers!" She gave a little giggle.

"Why should we?" asked Darrell, surprised. "We heard your old school had closed down. That was bad luck."

"Yes," said Maureen, and looked pensive. "It was such a marvellous school, too – you should have seen the playing fields! And we had two swimming pools, and were allowed to keep our own pets."

"Well, I expect you'll find Malory Towers isn't too bad," said Alicia, joining in.

"Oh *yes*," said the girl, smiling again, and showing her rabbit-teeth. "I'm sure it's *wonder*ful. That's why my mother chose it. She said that next to Mazeley Manor – that was my old school, you know – Malory Towers was the best."

"Dear me – that *was* nice of her," said Alicia in her smooth voice. "I don't seem to have heard of Mazeley Manor. Or was it the school whose girls always failed in the School Cert.?"

Maureen flushed. "Oh *no*," she said. "It couldn't have been. Why, quite half of us passed. I passed myself."

"Very clever of you," said Alicia, and Darrell nudged her. What a pity for Maureen to get on Alicia's wrong side so soon! She was just the type that irritated the sharp-tongued Alicia. Alicia winked at Darrell but Darrell frowned. It wasn't fair to tease a new girl so soon. Give her a chance!

But Maureen didn't give herself a chance! "I must be friendly!" she said to herself. "I must keep my own end up, I must im*press* these girls!"

So she chattered away in a light, airy voice, and didn't seem to realize that new girls should be seen and not heard! It was only when the others very pointedly began to talk to one another, turning away from her until she found that no one at all was listening to her, that she stopped.

In the first form if any new girl behaved like that the first-formers would have pointed out at once that she'd better keep her mouth shut before somebody sat on her. But the fifth-formers were not quite so crude. They merely ignored her, hoping she would see that she was behaving stupidly and making a bad start.

"Are we all back?" said Darrell, looking round the table. "Ah, there's Mavis. How's the voice, Mavis? I hope it's quite all right now!"

Mavis nodded. She had a beautiful voice, which she had lost for a few terms, but which was now back in all its beauty. She looked happy.

"And there's Mary-Lou – and Daphne – and Ruth – hallo, Ruth! How's your twin?"

"All right. You know she's been left down in fourth form?" said Ruth. "It'll be odd without her. I've always had her, no matter what school or form I've been in. I hope she won't miss me too much."

"Oh, she'll soon find someone else to look after and speak up for, just as she used to do to you!" said Alicia. "You were her little shadow, Ruth – now this term we'll be able to see what you're really like yourself. We didn't know before!"

"Oh!" put in Maureen, "is Ruth a twin? There were twins at my old school, and they were so . . . "

Well, it simply wasn't *done* for a new girl to speak out of turn like this, and to Maureen's surprise everyone at the table began talking at once, so that nobody could possibly hear what she said. Mam'zelle Dupont, who was at the head of the table, was sorry for her. She liked the fluffy type of girl, and she spoke comfortingly to Maureen.

"They are excited, you see, at being back again. You will soon be their friend, *n'est ce pas*? Tomorrow they will – what do you call it – they will take you to their chests and you will be one of them. What a pity dear Gwendoline isn't back yet. Now you would like her, Maureen. She has golden hair, like you, and . . . "

Alicia caught part of this and winked at Sally. "I bet Gwendoline would be just the person for Maureen," she said. She raised her voice and spoke to Mam'zelle.

"What's happened to dear Gwendoline Mary, Mam'zelle? She's the only one not back."

"She only came from France today," said Mam'zelle. "She comes to us tomorrow. The dear child – she will be able to talk to me about my beloved country. We shall gobble together about it."

"*Gabble*, Mam'zelle, you mean," said Sally, with a giggle.

"Oh, *I've* been to France, too," said Maureen, delighted.

"Then you and Gwendoline and Mam'zelle can all gobble about it together," said Irene. "Nice trio you'll make, gobbling away about *la belle* France!"

"Don't be an ass, Irene," said Moira's voice. "Remember you're in the fifth form now, not in the fourth."

"Oh – thanks most awfully for reminding us, Moira," said Alicia, in her smoothest voice. "I say – it must be *frightful* for you to have to live with *us* – awful come-down to pig it with old fourth-formers instead of queening it in the sixth."

"Moira and I don't mind a bit," said Catherine, with such an air of pouring oil on troubled waters that the old fourth-formers couldn't help nudging one another. "After all, *somebody* has to be left down sometimes – and it's always a help, don't you think, when an old member of the form can help new ones to carry on the tradition."

"*Ah ça – c'est bien dit!*" said Mam'zelle. "Very well said, Catherine."

But nobody else thought so. "Hypocrite!" muttered Alicia to Irene. "Who wants Catherine to help us? She couldn't teach a cat to drink milk! Gosh, if she's going to be as pi as that I shall resign from the fifth and go up into the sixth!"

Irene did one of her explosive snorts, and Catherine looked astonished. "Do tell us the joke," she said, with a beaming smile.

"Joke over," said Alicia, also with a beaming smile. Darrell winked at Sally. It was easy to see that there was going to be some fun that term. She glanced at Moira who was frowning glumly.

"Want to collect a few more scowls for your note-book, Belinda?" said Darrell, softly. Belinda glanced at Moira too and nodded. She had pursued Gwendoline once for a whole term, collecting her scowls, drawing them one after another in what the girls came to call her "Gwendoline Collection". Now here was another person with a wonderful selection of scowls for Belinda!

Bill and Clarissa were happily talking horses together, unheedful of anyone else at the table. "I wonder they don't whinny to one another!" said Alicia, exasperated. "Bill! Clarissa! Do you think you're in the stables still?"

"Oh – sorry," said Clarissa, looking round with shining green eyes. "I forgot where I was for a minute. But it's so nice to be back with Bill again and talk horses."

"Ah, this horse-talk! I do not understand it!" chimed in Mam'zelle. "Me, I would not go near a horse – great, stamping creatures."

"You really *must* come and let Thunder take a lump of sugar from the palm of your hand one day!" said Bill, with an impish grin. "Will you, Mam'zelle?"

Mam'zelle gave a small squeal. "Always you say that to me, Bill! It is not kind. I will not let your great horse tread on my foot with its paws."

"Hooves, Mam'zelle, hooves," said Bill, quite shocked at Mam'zelle calling them paws.

"Shaking its hair all over me," went on Mam'zelle,

conjuring up a fearsome picture of a stamping, head-shaking, rearing creature!

"Shaking its *mane*," corrected Bill. "Oh, Mam'zelle, you're awful about horses. I shall drag you out to Thunder and give you a lesson on all his different parts!"

"This horrible Bill!" said Mam'zelle, turning her eyes up to the ceiling. "Why must I teach her French when all she wants to learn about is horses? Why do you laugh, girls? I would not make a joke about so serious a thing!"

"Oh – it's good to back again, isn't it?" said Darrell to Sally. "I never laugh anywhere like I do at school, never!"

Night and Morning

Darrell found time that first evening to make sure that her young sister was not being whisked off by June, Alicia's thirteen-year-old cousin in the first form. To her relief she saw that Felicity was arm in arm with Susan, her friend of the term before.

June was standing alone, on the edge of the little crowd of first-formers. She had a most determined look on her face, and Darrell wondered what she was thinking of. "She is certainly planning *some*thing," thought Darrell. "Well, so long as she leaves Felicity out of her plans, she can do what she likes! How I do dislike that child!"

The fifth-formers went to bed a quarter of an hour after the fourth-formers. It was grand having just fifteen minutes more. They chattered as they undressed, and speculated on all sorts of things in the coming term.

"I shall miss having Miss Williams to teach us," said Sally, who had liked the fourth-form mistress very much. "I wonder if . . . "

The dormitory door opened and a face looked in. It was Connie, Ruth's twin.

"Ruth! Are you all right?" she said. "It's funny not being with you. Are you managing all right? Did you find your . . . "

"*Connie!*" exploded Alicia. "What do you mean by coming into the fifth dormy when you're jolly well supposed to be in bed? Clear out."

Connie stood in the doorway obstinately. She was a great one for arguing. "I only just came to see if Ruth was all right," she said. "We've never been parted before, and . . . "

"Clear out!" yelled everyone, and Irene brandished her hairbrush fiercely, almost knocking Belinda's eye out.

But still Connie held her ground. Her eyes searched Ruth's face, which was also wearing an obstinate look. "Ruth," began Connie, urgently. "Do say something. Don't stand there like that. I only just came to . . . "

"Clear out!" said Ruth, and everyone stood silent in astonishment. Nobody had expected that. Ruth had been such a shadow that, even when she had begun to assert herself a little the term before, no one had ever thought she could possibly order Connie about.

"I know you're my twin and we've always been together," said Ruth, in an unnecessarily loud voice. "But I'm in the fifth now and you're in the fourth. You can't come tagging after a fifth-former, you know that. Leave me alone and clear out!"

Only Ruth could defeat Connie, and make her go. Connie gaped, then turned and went without a word.

Ruth sat down suddenly on her bed.

"Good for *you*!" said Darrell, warmly. "You'll have to stand up for yourself a bit, Ruth, or you'll have Connie pestering you again and again."

"I know," said Ruth in a small voice. "But I'm – I'm awfully fond of her, you know – I hated saying that. But she would never take any notice of anyone else. And after all – I can't let her hang on to the fifth, can I? Poor Connie."

"Not 'poor' at all," said Darrell. "And don't you believe it. She's got the cheek of a dozen! She won't give up easily, either – she'll keep on trying to tag on to you and to us."

"Quite right," said Alicia, in a voice not loud enough for Ruth to hear. "Connie's so thickskinned she wants a whole lot of pummelling and shouting at before she feels or understands what we're getting at!"

"I've got a sister like that in the fourth," said Moira, unexpectedly joining in. "A tough nut if ever there was one. She's like a rubber ball – if you sit on her and squash her flat she bounces back to shape immediately. Awful kid."

"What's her name?" said Darrell. "Oh, wait a bit – is it Bridget?"

"Yes," said Moira. "She and Connie would make a pair!"

"Well, let's hope Connie and she will get together!" said Alicia. "Nice pair they'd make – rub each other's corners off a bit!"

Soon they were all in bed. Darrell was next to Maureen. She said goodnight to the new girl, and to Sally who was on the other side of her, and shut her eyes. Her bed was harder than at home but she knew she would soon get used to that. She threw off her eiderdown after a bit. It was such a warm night. She heard a sniff from the next bed.

"Gosh – it can't be Maureen sniffing like any first-former," thought Darrell, in surprise. She turned over and listened.

"Sniff, sniff!" Yes, there it was again.

"Maureen! What on earth's the matter?" whispered Darrell. "Surely you're not a first-night sniffer? At *your* age?"

Maureen's voice came shakily to Darrell. "I'm always like this at first. I think of Mother and Daddy and what they're doing at home. I'm sensitive, you know."

"Better get over being sensitive then," said Darrell, shortly. In her experience people who went round saying that they were sensitive wanted a good shaking up, and, if they were lower school, needed to be laughed out of it.

"But you can't help being it, if you are," sniffed Maureen.

"Oh, I know – but you *can* help talking about it!" said Darrell. "Do go to sleep. I can't bear to hear you sniffing as if you wanted a hanky and haven't got one."

Maureen felt that Darrell was very unkind. She wished there was someone in the bed the other side of her – someone more sympathetic. But the bed was empty. It was Gwendoline's and she hadn't yet come back.

Darrell grinned to herself in the darkness. If only they could wish Maureen on to Gwen! Maureen was very like Gwen to look at, and had the same silly weak nature, apparently. How marvellous if they could push her on to Gwen, and see what happened!

"You wait till Gwendoline Mary comes back tomorrow," said Darrell wickedly to Maureen. "She's just your sort. She's sensitive, too. I'm sure she'll understand all you feel. She hates first nights still. You look out for her tomorrow, Maureen, she's just your sort, I should think."

Sally, who was in the next bed, listening, gave a little snort of laughter. How mad Gwen would be to have someone else like her in the form, someone who thought themselves too wonderful for words, and who wanted admiration and sympathy all the time! How wicked of Darrell to be pushing Maureen on to Gwen already – but how altogether suitable!

"No more talking," said Moira's voice, out of the darkness. "Time's up now."

The old fourth-formers resented this sudden command. Moira wasn't head girl – not yet, anyway! Nothing official had been said about it. Nobody said any more but there were various "Poohs" and "Pishes" from several beds. Still, they were all tired, and nobody except Maureen really wanted to keep awake.

There were a few more sniffs from Maureen's bed and then silence. Irene began to snore a little. She always did when she lay on her back. Belinda, who was in the next bed, leaned over and gave her a hard poke to make her turn over. Irene obediently shifted on to her side without even waking up. Belinda had got her well trained by now!

Connie actually appeared at the door again in the morning, looking belligerent and obstinate.

"You *still* there?" said Alicia. "Been standing there all night long, I suppose, wondering if Ruth was having a nice beauty sleep or not!"

"There's no rule against my coming here in the morning to ask a question, is there?" said Connie. "Don't be so beastly, Alicia. I've only come to give Ruth a pair of stockings that got into my case."

"Thanks," said Ruth, and took them. Connie straightened one or two things on Ruth's dressing table. Ruth immediately put them crooked again. "It's

28

no good, Connie," she said. "Leave me alone. I'm in the fifth now, I tell you."

"I never thought you'd crow over me if I was left behind," said Connie, looking suddenly bewildered.

"I'm not. Do go away," said Ruth, in a low voice, knowing that everyone in the room was intensely interested in this little battle, although most of the girls were pretending not to notice. Darrell had managed to stop Alicia from interfering. Let Ruth manage the fight herself!

Moira suddenly spoke. "Will you take this book to my sister Bridget?" she said, in her abrupt voice. She held out a small book. "She's in the fourth, too – came up from the third this term. I expect you've spoken to her already."

"Yes, I have," said Connie. "I'll give her the book."

She took it, and went out of the room without another look at Ruth. Darrell glanced at Ruth. She was looking rather miserable. What a shame it was that Connie should force her into such a difficult position! How could anyone be as thickskinned as that twin!

The breakfast bell went. Maureen gave a wail. "Oh, I say – is that the bell again? I was thinking I was still at Mazeley Manor – the bell didn't go till much later! I shall be late!"

"We're going to hear rather a lot about Mazeley Manor, I'm afraid," said Darrell in Sally's ear, as they went downstairs.

"Perhaps Gwen will hear it all instead," said Sally. "That's your plan, isn't it? The thing is – will Gwen be in the fifth? *She* failed the School Cert., too, you know. She maybe kept down in the fourth with Connie."

"Oh no – surely not!" said Darrell. "She's too old. She's above the average age even of the fifth, by a few months. After all, Connie's well below it – so it doesn't much matter for her."

They asked Mam'zelle at breakfast time about Gwen.

"Will she be in the fifth with us?" said Darrell.

"Yes, yes," said Mam'zelle. "Of course! It is true she failed, the poor child, in this terrible examination of yours – but she was ill. Yes, she had a bad heart, poor Gwendoline."

The fifth-formers nudged one another. Gwen's bad heart! Gwen had produced a heart that fluttered and palpitated, in order to get out of doing the exam – but nobody had believed in it except Mam'zelle. And Gwen had had to do the exam after all, and failed.

"Well, heart or no heart, apparently she's in the fifth with us," said Alicia. "*Dear* Gwendoline Mary – *what* a treat to have her back with us today!"

Miss James has Good News

The fifth went to their classroom just before nine o'clock. They rejoiced in the glorious view. Darrell flung the windows wide and let in the golden September air.

"Heavenly!" she said. "I hope we shall be allowed to bathe still. I bet the pool down in the rocks is just perfect now."

Maureen looked alarmed. "Surely you're not allowed to bathe in the winter term!" she said. "Why, at Mazeley Manor we . . . "

"It must have been a wonderful place," said Alicia, in her smooth voice.

"Oh yes – we used to . . . " went on Maureen.

"*So* sad it had to shut down," interrupted Irene.

"Yes, very sad," agreed Maureen, delighted at this sudden interest and sympathy. "You see, all of us were very . . ."

"You must find Malory Towers very second rate after such a marvellous place," put in Belinda, also sounding very sympathetic.

"Still, we'll do our best," Sally assured her. Maureen began to feel doubtful about all these interruptions, kind as they seemed. Perhaps she had better say no more till she had found her feet a little? These girls seemed so different from the ones at dear Mazeley Manor.

"What's our new form mistress, Miss James, like?" said Darrell to Catherine and Moira. "You've been taught by her for some terms – is she all right?"

"Easygoing to a point," said Moira. "Then look out! She changes from sweet to sour in the twinkling of an eye – and it's bad for you if you don't notice the changeover immediately. Still, Jimmy's not a bad sort."

"She's James when she's sour, and Jimmy when she's sweet," explained Catherine, with her beaming smile. "Actually she's rather a dear."

"Oh, Catherine thinks heaps of people are 'rather-dears', and 'dear-old-souls' and even 'pet-lambs'," said Moira. "She never speaks evil of anyone, do you, Catherine? And if ever you want anything done, Catherine will do it for you – she just loves to run around for other people."

Catherine blushed. "Don't be silly, Moira," she said, but a look of anxiety came into her eyes. Was Moira pulling her leg – sneering at her just a little? The others didn't wonder about it – they knew! Moira was not praising Catherine – she was sneering. Moira would probably never praise anyone wholeheartedly.

The girls had chosen their desks. The favoured

ones at the back of the room went to the two old fifth-formers, of course, Moira and Catherine, and to Darrell and Sally, who had each been head girl for a time the term before. Irene and Belinda also had desks in the back row.

There were other girls in the room now, girls also in the fifth but from other Towers – Tessa and Janet and Penelope, Katie and Dora and Gladys – girls the North Tower fifth-formers knew by name and sight, but not nearly as well as they knew their own Tower girls, of course. The girls of all the Towers mixed for lessons and games, but were quite separate afterwards, each going to their own Tower for meals, leisure and sleeping.

"Sssssst!" said someone. "Jimmy's coming!"

And in came Jimmy, or Miss James – a tall, spare woman of about fifty, whose curly grey hair framed a scholarly face with kind but shrewd hazel eyes.

"Sit," she said, and the class sat, shuffling their feet, moving their chairs a little, shifting books and papers. Miss James waited until there was complete silence.

"Well, once more I have a new class," she began, her shrewd eyes resting first on one girl and then on another. "Only three of you, I think, were in my form last term, and they, for various good reasons, have not gone up into the sixth, but are still with me. They will, of course, be a great help in getting the form into my ways."

The girls looked to see who the third old fifth-former was. Oh – it was little Janet. Well, she was miles too young to go up into the sixth, of course! She had only been put into the fifth a year ago because she had passed her School Certificate so absurdly early. She still looked like a fourth-former, thought Darrell, not even like a fifth-former!

Janet looked pleased to be left down. She was scared

of the sixth form. Moira scowled. She hated being left behind. Catherine beamed. Yes – yes, she would help all she could. Miss James could depend on her, of course she could. She tried to catch the mistress's eye, but for some reason Miss James steadfastly looked in the other direction.

Catherine kept her beaming smile on for some time, hopefully gazing at Miss James. But the mistress left the subject and began on something else. Catherine had to switch off the smile. Her cheek muscles were beginning to ache!

"Darrell is to be head of fifth-form games," said Miss James. "Sally is to help her. You realize, Darrell, don't you, that head of fifth-form games means taking on the training of some of the younger players for the lower teams of the school? That will take up some time, but you will have Sally to help you."

Darrell glowed. How lovely to be able to pick out some of the young first and second-formers and lick them into shape for the Third and Fourth Games Teams of Malory Towers. Suppose she and Sally made the teams so good that they won all their matches, home and away! What a record that would be! Darrell went off into a day-dream in which she saw some well-turned out, smart lower-school teams winning match after match.

"I'll train Felicity, of course," she thought. "She's quite good already. I can make her first class. And Susan's good as well. And I'll lick that young June into shape, too. My word, she'll have to toe the line now. I shan't stand any nonsense from *her*! And there's Harriet in the second form and Lucy in the second, too . . ."

She missed the next few things that Miss James said, she was so lost in her dream of first-class lacrosse teams.

"You all worked very hard last term," said Miss James. "Practically all of you in this form passed, and passed well, in the School Cert. exam. Those who didn't failed because of some understandable reason, and will have another chance later on. They will be specially coached for it, and will have to leave the usual lessons of this class for a time until the exam is over."

Alicia sighed. It wouldn't be this term of course – but she hated the idea of having to leave the others and have special coaching. Blow! Why did she have to have measles right in exam week last term?

"Now, as you all had a hard term last term, I don't intend to work you hard *this* term," said Miss James, and a sigh of relief went all round the room like a small breeze. "I mean – I shall not set you lengthy preps to do, nor push you hard – but there will be other things to take up your time. I want the fifth to produce the Christmas entertainment this year, for instance."

That made everyone sit up. Produce the Christmas entertainment! My word! That would be fun. What about a play? Or a pantomime? Or a ballet? All kinds of thoughts ran through the girls' minds, and they glanced at one another in delight.

"You will do it all on your own, except for any advice you may need from Mr Young, the music master, or Miss Greening, the elocution coach," went on Miss James, pleased at the pleasure shown by the girls. Ah, when they got up into the fifth, how they liked to do things on their own, with no interference from anyone! Quite right, too – if they didn't learn to handle affairs and stand on their own feet now, they never would!

"You will choose your own producers," said Miss James. "I should have at least two, for the work will be too much for one. The more you do on your own the better I and Miss Grayling, the head, will be pleased – but we shall, of course, be glad to give you any advice or help if you need to ask for it."

Every girl in the class at once fiercely determined not to ask for one single piece of advice. The Christmas Show, whatever it was, should be theirs and nobody else's.

"It shall be the best one ever done at Malory Towers!" vowed Darrell.

"We'll get the parents to come and what a surprise they'll have!" thought Sally.

"What a chance!" thought Alicia, and her agile mind began to run over all kinds of ideas at once. She longed for the first meeting. If only they would make her one of the producers! She could organize well. She could plan and she could be more resourceful than anyone. She knew she could!

They all longed for Break, so that they could discuss the ideas put into their heads by Miss James. Irene was in the seventh heaven of delight – if they did a pantomime, *would* they let her write the music? The music for a whole pantomime – why, that would give her more scope than she had ever had before!

Mavis was also dreaming delightfully. Would she be able to do some of the singing, if they did a play or a pantomime? She was allowed to practise her singing properly this term, and had a special singing master of her own, who came to the school to teach her. Oh, if only she could sing the principal songs!

Break came at last. The fifth-formers rushed off in a crowd, gathering in a corner of the grounds, all talking at once.

"We'll have to have a proper meeting," said Darrell. "Oh gosh – I do feel thrilled – to be told we can do the Christmas entertainment all on our own – and to be told I'm Games Captain and responsible for the picking and training of the lower-school kids for their teams! Why – I shan't have time for any work at all!"

"Well, we've learnt how to work by now," said Sally. "If we haven't we never will! We've got other things to learn now, I suppose – how to plan things on our own, and carry them out – and how to work together in them properly – things like that."

"Oh! Do you suppose Jimmy's planned all this just to make us learn a whole lot of *other* things then?" said Daphne.

"Quite likely," said Alicia. "But what does it matter? If we're learning something by producing a pantomime, well, let's learn it by all means! I'm all for it!"

"We have to choose a committee," said Moira, taking charge. Sally, Darrell and Alicia felt a momentary annoyance. They had been so used to leading everything in the fourth form that they found it difficult to recognize Moira's authority. Still, she was head girl. She had the right to take charge, and she was perfectly capable of it – there was no doubt about that at all.

The girls could all feel the impact of a hard and dominating personality in Moira – much the same as they felt in Alicia, who was also hard and strong in character. But Alicia had a sense of humour, which was quite lacking in Moira – that made all the difference in the world!

Alicia could say something biting – and yet it would produce a laugh because of the way she said it. She was jolly and lively, too, which Moira was not. Well, it took all sorts to make a world, and there was a place for the Moiras and Gwens and Maureens, thought Darrell, and for the Sallies and Irenes and Belindas as well.

"Only *they're* so much nicer to know!" Darrell said to herself.

"We'd better choose a committee of seven or eight,"

36

went on Moira. "And we'll choose it in the usual way – each of us writes the names of the girls they'd like to have on the committee and we'll put them all into a box. Then we take them out, open them, count them, and see who's got the most votes. We'll do that tonight."

"Oh, I *hope* I'm on the committee!" thought Darrell. And Alicia hoped the same. Alicia badly wanted to have a finger in this pie. She felt perfectly sure she could run the whole show, if only she was allowed to!

Half an hour in the Sun

"When's dear Gwendoline Mary coming back?" asked Alicia, as they all lay out in the sun after their lunch at a quarter to two that day. It was so warm and sunny that it was like summer. All the girls had found warm places out of doors, and the grounds were full of little companies of girls happily sunning themselves.

"Gwen? Oh, she's arriving at tea time," said Darrell. "*Dear* Gwendoline Mary! Would you think she's what Catherine would call a 'pet lamb'?"

"I could think of much more suitable names than that," said Belinda, busy drawing Mavis, who had gone to sleep with her mouth open.

"Is Gwendoline nice?" asked Maureen. "She *sounds* nice, to me."

Darrell winked at Alicia.

"Nice? Oh, you'll love her!" she said. "*So* sympathetic and ready to listen! So interesting to talk to – and the tales she tells about her family and her dogs and her cats – well, you could listen for hours, Maureen."

"Is she fond of sports?" asked Maureen, who quite definitely wasn't. "At Mazeley Manor we didn't do games unless we wanted to. I mean – they weren't compulsory, as they are here – *such* a mistake, I think."

"Oh, Gwen hates games," said Alicia. "But because she's fat she has to do them as much as possible and walk miles, too."

"Poor Gwendoline!" said Maureen, sympathizing deeply with the absent fifth-former. "We shall have a lot in common, I can see. Has she – has she a special friend, do you know? Of course – that's a silly question I know – a girl like that's bound to have a special friend. But I just thought – you know, I'm rather one on my own – it would be so *nice* to find someone here who wasn't already fixed up with a companion for walks – and talks."

"Let me see," said Alicia, blinking up at the sky. "*Has* Gwendoline Mary a friend?"

Everyone appeared to think very deeply.

"Well – perhaps not a *special* friend," said Irene, with a small snort of laughter. "Let us say she's a little-friend-of-all-the-world, shall we?"

"Ah – you've just hit the nail on the head," said Darrell, trying not to giggle. "I think she'd like Maureen, don't you?"

"She'll love her," said Belinda, with the utmost conviction. "Wake up, Mavis, and see how beautiful you look when you're asleep."

"Beast!" said Mavis, taking a look at Belinda's comical sketch of her lying asleep with her mouth open. Maureen took a look as well.

"That's quite a clever drawing," she said. "I can draw, too. I was one of the best at Mazeley Manor. I must show you my sketches sometime, Belinda.

38

They're very much the same style as yours."

Belinda was about to say something short and rude when Irene frowned at her, and then spoke in a sickly-sweet tone to the unsuspecting Maureen.

"I suppose you can sing, too, can't you – and can you compose?"

"Oh, I can sing," said Maureen, pleased with all this attention. "Yes, I had special lessons at Mazeley Manor. The singing master said I had a most unusual voice. And I've composed quite a few songs. Dear, dear – you mustn't make me talk about myself like this!"

She gave her silly little laugh. Everyone else wanted to laugh, too. How could anyone be so idiotic?

"Were there many girls at your last school?" asked Sally, wondering how in the world any school could turn out somebody like Maureen.

"Oh no – it was a very very *select* school," said Maureen. "They picked and chose their girls very very carefully."

"You'll have to tell Gwen all these things," said Alicia, earnestly. "Won't she, girls? Gwen will be *so* interested. And don't you think it would be nice for dear Gwendoline to have someone like Maureen for a friend? I mean – I feel she's made of, er – finer stuff than we are – and I'm sure Gwendoline Mary would appreciate that."

Maureen could hardly believe that all these wonder-full remarks applied to her. She gazed round half-suspiciously, but the girls all looked at her with straight faces. Irene had to look away. She felt certain one of her terrific snorts was coming.

"Gwen's always lonely when she comes back," went on Alicia. "Then's the time to talk to her, Maureen. We'll tell her about you, and you can make friends."

"Thank you very much," said Maureen, basking in what she thought was universal appreciation of herself.

"I really hardly think the girls at Mazeley Manor could be nicer than you!"

Irene snorted loudly and somehow turned it into a cough and a sneeze.

Maureen looked a little suspicious again, but at that moment Mam'zelle Dupont descended on them, smiling. She sat down on the grass, first looking for ants, earwigs and beetles. She was terrified of them. She beamed round amicably. The girls smiled back. They liked the plump, hot tempered, humorous French mistress. She was not like Mam'zelle Rougier, bad tempered all the time – if she got into a temper, she blew up, certainly – but it didn't last long.

"Ah – you are all basketing in the sun," she said, much to the surprise of everyone.

"Oh – you mean *basking*, don't you, Mam'zelle?" said Darrell, with a squeal of laughter.

"Yes, yes – this lovely sun!" said Mam'zelle, and she wriggled her plump shoulders in enjoyment. In a moment or two, however, she would feel afraid of getting a freckle, and would retire into the shade!

"And you, *ma petite* Maureen – you are settling down here nicely, are you not?" asked Mam'zelle, kindly, seeing Maureen next to her. "Of course, you will be missing your old school – what name is it, now – ah, yes – your Measley Manor, is it not?"

A shout of laughter deafened her.

"Oh, Mam'zelle – you're priceless!" almost wept Belinda. "You always hit the nail on the head!"

"The nail? What nail?" asked Mam'zelle, looking all round as if she expected to see a nail suspended in the air somewhere. "I have hit nothing. Do not tease me now. It is too hot!"

She turned to Maureen again. "They interrupt their kind old Mam'zelle," she said, smiling down at the fluffy-haired Maureen. "I was asking you about your lovely Measley Manor."

This time it was too much. Maureen's look of offended disgust with Mam'zelle and with the laughing girls made them roll on the grass in an agony of mirth. Mam'zelle was astonished. What had she said that was so funny?

"All I ask is about this lovely . . . " she began again, in bewilderment. Nobody stopped laughing. Maureen got up and walked off in a huff. How hateful to laugh at such a horrid name for her old school – and did Mam'zelle *really* mean to call it that? Was she poking fun at her, too? Maureen seriously began to doubt if all the nice things said to her were meant.

"Oh dear," said Darrell, sitting up and wiping the tears from her eyes. "You're a pet, Mam'zelle! Girls, in future, we refer to *Measley Manor* as soon as Maureen trots out her horrible soppy school again. We'll soon cure her of that."

"I wish Gwen would hurry up and come," said Sally. "I'm longing to see those two together. Maureen's so like Gwen in her ways – it'll be like Gwen looking into a mirror and seeing herself, when she knows Maureen!"

"Now, now – play no treeks on Maureen," said Mam'zelle. She meant tricks, of course. "Poof! It is hot. I shall grow a freckle on my nose. I feel it! I must sit in the shade. Poof!"

"We're going to have a nice term, Mam'zelle," said Darrell. "Games, plenty of them – and we fifth-formers are doing the Christmas entertainment! We shan't have much time for French, I'm afraid,"

"*Méchante fille*," said Mam'zelle at once, fanning violently and making herself much hotter. "Bad girl, Darrell. You will have plenty of time for French. And no treeks. No treeks this term. There will be NO TIME for treeks."

41

"Why don't *you* play a treek, Mam'zelle?" asked Alicia, lazily. "We give you full permission to work as hard as you like at playing a treek on us."

"Oh yes – as many tricks as you like!" said Sally, joyfully.

"But we'll see through them all," said Mavis.

"Ah – if I played you a treek it would be *superbe!*" said Mam'zelle, pronouncing it the French way, "*Superbe! Magnifique! Merveilleuse!* Such a treek you would never have seen before."

"We dare you to, Mam'zelle," said Alicia at once.

"Me, I am not daring," said Mam'zelle. "I think of a treek perhaps, yes – but I could not do it. *Hèlas*! I have not your dare."

The bell rang for afternoon school. Everyone got up. Alicia hauled Mam'szelle to her feet so strongly that she almost fell over again. "You have too much dare," she told Alicia, crossly. "Always you have much dare, Alicia!"

Gwendoline Arrives

Gwendoline came back just before tea, by car. The news flew round. "Dear Gwendoline Mary's back! Come and see the fond farewells!"

Gwen's farewells were a standing joke at Malory Towers. There were always tears and fond embracings, and injunctions to write soon, that went on for ages between her and her mother and her old governess, Miss Winter, who lived with them.

Faces lined the windows overlooking the drive. Gwendoline got out of the car. Her mother and Miss

Winter got out, too. Her father, who was driving, made no move. He had got very tired of Gwendoline in the holidays.

"Out come the hankies!" said Alicia, and out came Gwen's and her mother's and Miss Winter's. And dear me, out came the hankies of all the wicked watchers at the windows above!

"Now we pat our eyes!" went on Alicia, and sure enough the eye-patting went on down below – and above too, as everyone sniffed and wiped their eyes.

Irene, of course, gave the show away with one of her explosions. The four below looked up in surprise and saw the watching girls, all with hankies to their eyes.

Mr Lacy roared. He held on to the wheel and laughed loudly. "They're putting up as good a show for you, Gwen, as you're putting up for them!" he cried. The girls at the window disappeared as soon as they saw that they had been seen. They felt a little uncomfortable. Mrs Lacy might complain of their bad manners now! It would be just like her.

"Mother, get back into the car," said Gwendoline exasperated. She hadn't known she was being watched at all. She did so love these little farewell scenes – and now this one was spoilt! Her mother and Miss Winter were almost hustled back, without another tear or hug.

"I don't like that behaviour, Gwendoline," said Mrs Lacy, offended at the conduct of the girls. "I've a good mind to write to Miss Grayling."

"Oh *no*, Mother!" said Gwendoline, in alarm. She never liked being brought to Miss Grayling's notice at all. Miss Grayling had said some very horrid things to her at times!

"It's all right, Gwen. I shan't let her," said her father, dryly. "For goodness' sake, say goodbye now, and go in. And mind – if I hear any nonsense about

43

you this term you'll have me to reckon with, not your mother. You were bad and foolish last term, and you suffered for it. You will suffer for it again, if I hear bad reports of you. On the other hand, no one will be more pleased than I shall to have a good report of you. And I've no doubt I shall."

"Yes, Daddy," said Gwendoline, meekly.

"How unkind you are just as we're leaving Gwen," said Mrs Lacy, dabbing her eyes again. "Goodbye, darling. I shall miss you so!"

Gwendoline took a desperate look up at the windows. Gracious, was Mother going to begin all over again?

"Goodbye," she said, curtly, and shut the car door. Immediately her father put in the clutch and the car moved off. Without even turning to wave Gwen marched up the steps with her lacrosse stick and night case. Her trunk had been sent on in advance.

Maureen had not seen the fond farewells. She did not see Gwen till tea time. Gwen took her case up to the dormy and was thankful to find it empty. She looked at herself in the glass. She wasn't fat any more – well, not *very*, she decided. All those hateful walks had taken away her weight. And now she had to face a term with heaps of games and walks – but thank goodness, no swimming!

The tea bell went. Gwen quickly brushed her fluffy golden hair, so like Maureen's, washed her hands, pulled her tie straight, and went downstairs.

She walked into the dining room with the last few girls. She caught sight of her form at the fifth-form table. They waved to her.

"Hallo! Here's dear Gwendoline Mary again!"

"Had good hols?"

"You went to France, didn't you? Lucky thing!"

"Said goodbye to your parents?"

Gwendoline felt pleased to be back. Of course, it *was* nice to be at home with her mother and Miss Winter and be waited on hand and foot, and be fussed over – but it was fun at school. She made up her mind to be sensible and join in everything this term. So she smiled round very amiably.

"Hallo, everyone! It's nice to be back. You'll have to tell me all the news. I only got back from France yesterday."

"Ah – *la belle* France!" put in Mam'zelle. "We must have some chest-to-chest talks about *la belle* France."

Gwen looked surprised. "Oh – you mean heart-to-heart talks, Mam'zelle. Yes, that would be lovely."

"Gwendoline, there's a new girl," said Alicia, in a suspiciously smooth voice. "Let me introduce her – you'll like her. This is Maureen. And this is Gwendoline Mary. A bit alike to look at, aren't they, Mam'zelle?"

"*C'est vrai!*" agreed Mam'zelle. "Yes, it is true. Both so golden – and with big blue eyes. Ah yes, it is a true English beauty, that!"

This gratified both Gwen and Maureen immensely, and made them look with great interest at each other. They shook hands and smiled.

"I've kept a place for you," said Maureen, shyly, making her eyes big as she looked at Gwen. Gwen sat down and looked to see what there was for tea. She was hungry after her long car journey.

"Have some of my honey," said Maureen, eagerly. "We keep bees, you know – and we always have *such* a lot of honey. We have hens, too. So we have plenty of eggs. I brought some back with me. I hope you'll share them with me."

Gwendoline rather liked all this. Dear me, she

must have made quite an impression on the new girl, although she had only just arrived!

"The others have been telling me about you," gushed Maureen. "How popular you seem to be!"

This didn't ring quite true, somehow, to Gwendoline. She hadn't known she was as popular as all that. In fact, though she didn't admit it frankly to herself, she knew quite well she was probably the least popular of all the girls in the form!

Maureen chattered away merrily, and Gwen listened, not so much because she wanted to, as because she was so busy tucking in. At this rate, thought the amused Alicia, Gwendoline would put on more fat than games and gym and walks would take off!

"You'll be pleased to hear we haven't got to work quite so hard this term, Gwen," she told her. "More time for games and gym. You'll like that."

Gwendoline gave Alicia one of her Looks, as she called them. Alas, they never impressed Alicia. It wasn't safe to argue with Alicia, or contradict, or try to say something cutting. Alicia was always ten times as quick at answering back and a hundred times as cutting as anyone else.

"We'll have the committee meeting at half past five," announced Moira. "That seems to be the best time. You'll be coming, Gwendoline, won't you – have you heard about the Christmas Entertainment Committee yet?"

Gwendoline hadn't, so she was duly enlightened. She was pleased. She saw herself at once in one of the chief parts of whatever play or pantomime was chosen. She would loosen her sheet of golden hair – what a pity it wasn't curly. She would look lovely, she knew she would!

Exactly the same thoughts were going through Maureen's mind. She too would like one of the chief parts – and she too would play it with her golden hair loose. She felt she would like to confide her thoughts to Gwendoline.

"When I was at Mazeley Manor," she began. Belinda interrupted at once.

"Oh yes – have you told Gwen about Measley Manor?"

Maureen frowned. "You know it's *Mazeley*," she said, with dignity. "Mam'zelle just didn't know how to pronounce it, that's all, when she said it."

Mam'zelle caught her name mentioned. She turned, with her wide smile. "Ah – you want to talk about Measley Manor again, your dear old school, *n'est-ce pas*? You have not yet told Gwendoline about Measley Manor?"

Maureen saw the girls grinning and gave it up. She went on talking to Gwen, who was astonished at all this by-play which she didn't, of course, understand.

"At my old school we did a pantomime," said Maureen. "It was 'Sleeping Beauty'. I had to have my hair loose, of course. You *have* to have someone with golden hair for those parts, don't you?"

Gwen agreed heartily. She was very proud of her golden hair, and only wished she was allowed to wear it loose round her face at school, as she did at home.

"The prince was grand," went on Maureen. "I really must tell you all about the play. You're so interested in plays, aren't you? Well . . . "

And till long past tea time Maureen went on and on interminably with her long and boring tale of what happened in the play at her last school. Gwendoline couldn't stop her or get rid of her. Maureen was just as thickskinned and slow at taking a hint as she was!

"Gwen's met her match at last," said Darrell to Sally. "I say, look at Bill – and Clarissa, too – all dressed up in riding things. Don't they *know* the committee meeting's in about ten minutes?"

Sally called to them. "Hey, you two! Where do you think you're going?"

"To have a look at Thunder and Merrylegs," said Bill.

"But didn't you *know* there's a committee meeting on almost at once?" said Darrell, exasperated.

"No. Nobody told us," said Clarissa, looking startled. "It wasn't up on the notice board."

"Well, we've been talking about it ever since this morning, and except for Maureen and Gwen, who discussed golden-haired beauties in plays, we've talked about nothing else all tea time," said Darrell. "Where are your ears? Didn't you hear a word of it?"

"Not a word," said Bill, seriously. "I'm so sorry. Of course we'll come. Have we time just to go and see Thunder and Merrylegs first? We must have been talking about something else, Clarissa and I, and not heard the rest of you."

"You were whinnying away to each other," said Sally. "I suppose you've got horses on the brain again. No, don't go down to the stables now – you certainly won't be back till the end of the committee if you do. I know you two when you disappear into the stables. You're gone for ever!"

Clarissa and Bill walked off to the fifth-form common room with a good grace. Perhaps there would be time afterwards to go to the stables.

"Come on," said Sally to Darrell. "Let's go and round up all the others. I'm longing for this committee."

Meeting at half past Five

The whole of the fifth form was soon collected in the North Tower common room. The girls sat on the chairs, lounged on the couches, or lay on the floor rugs. They talked and shouted and laughed. Moira came in and went straight to the table. A big chair had been put behind it.

Moira banged on the table with a book.

"Quiet!" she said. "The meeting is about to begin. You all know what it's about. It's to choose a committee to handle the organization of the Christmas entertainment, which we, the fifth form, are to undertake."

"Hear hear," said somebody's voice. Moira took no notice.

"I think the whole form should also be asked to discuss and choose what kind of entertainment we shall do," she said.

"Punch and Judy Show!" called someone.

"Don't be funny," said Moira. "Now, first of all we'll get down to the business of choosing the committee. I asked Catherine to cut out the slips of paper to use. Where are they, Catherine?"

She turned to where Catherine was sitting next to her. Catherine handed her a sheaf of slips.

"Here they are. I did them all as soon as you told me you wanted them. And here's a box. I got it out of the cupboard in the fifth-form room. And I've collected enough pencils for everyone to use. And look . . . "

"All right, all right," said Moira. "That's all we shall want. Now who'll give out the paper slips? You, Mary-Lou?"

Mary-Lou was perched upon the top of a small cupboard, swinging her legs. She made preparations to climb down.

"No, no – don't you bother, Mary-Lou," said Catherine, at once. "I'll give them out." And before anyone could stop her she was going round the room, handing everyone a slip of paper and a pencil.

"Everyone got a slip?" asked Moira. "Look, Mavis hasn't got one, Catherine."

"*So* sorry I missed you out!" said Catherine, in an apologetic voice. She always apologized if she could. "Here you are."

"Now," said Moira, "I think we'll have eight people on this committee – because there will be a lot of work to be done. We shall want someone to represent the art side, for instance – someone for the music side – and so on. I must be one of the committee, as I am head girl, so you need not vote for me, of course. That means you need only put down seven names."

"Well, I don't know that I *should* have voted for Moira," said Alicia to Irene, in a low voice. "Too bossy for my taste. We shall all have to salute her when we meet her soon!"

Everyone was soon busy scribbling down names. Maureen was at a loss because she knew so few. Gwendoline prompted her, and Moira soon noticed it.

"Gwendoline! Don't tell Maureen names to put down. That simply means *you* have two votes instead of one. I forgot that Maureen is new. We shall have to leave her out of this for the moment."

The papers were folded over and put into the box

that Catherine took round. Then, whilst the rest of the girls chattered, Moira and Catherine took out the slips, jotted ticks beside the names of the girls chosen, and counted them up.

Moira rapped on the table. "Silence, please! We've got the results now. These are the names of the girls with most votes: Alicia, Mavis, Irene, Belinda, Darrell, Janet – and Sally and Betty tie."

Janet and Betty were girls from other houses who were in the fifth form. Betty was Alicia's best friend, as clever and witty as she was, and very popular.

"Well, there you are," said Moira. "As Sally and Betty have tied, we'd better have them both in, making a committee of nine, instead of eight."

"I'll take on the music side," said Irene.

"And I'd like to take the art side – any decorations and so on," said Belinda.

"I draw very well," whispered Maureen to Gwen. "I could help with that. Shall I say so?"

"No," said Gwen, who couldn't draw anything, and didn't particularly want this new girl to shine.

"I'll take on the costumes," said Janet, who was extremely clever with her needle, and made all her own dresses. "I'd love to help with those."

"Good," said Moira, approvingly.

"Could I – do you think I could help with the *singing* part of it?" said Mavis, hesitatingly. "I don't want to push myself forward – but if there's to be any singing – you know, choruses and all that – I could train them. I've had such a lot of training myself I think I'd know how to set about it."

"Right. That's a good idea," said Moira.

"And if there's any solo work, you can sing it yourself!" called Darrell. "Your voice is lovely now."

Mavis flushed with pleasure. "Oh well – I'll see.

51

There might not be any," she said. "It depends what we do, doesn't it?"

"That leaves Alicia, Darrell, Sally and myself for general things – the organization," said Moira, who was certainly able to handle a meeting well, and make it get on with things. "We'll have to work together smoothly, efficiently – and amicably."

She glanced at Alicia, as she spoke, a quick, rather hostile glance, a mere flick of the eyes. But Alicia caught it and noted it. That word "amicably" was meant for her. All right – she would be amicable just as long as Moira was – and not a moment longer!

"Well, now that we've got the members of the committee settled, we'll get on with the next thing," said Moira. "What kind of entertainment shall we give?"

"Pantomime!"

"No – a play – a humorous play! Let's do 'A Quiet Week-End'!"

"A variety show!"

"A ballet! Oh, do let's do a ballet!"

The last suggestion was from a girl who was a beautiful ballet dancer. She was cried down.

"No, no – that's too one-sided. We can't all dance!"

"Well, let's have something that everyone can be in, and *do* something in."

"Well, it had better be a pantomime then," said Moira. "We can have songs, dances, acting and all kinds of sideshows in that. A pantomime never sticks to its story – it just does what it likes."

After some more shouting and discussion a pantomime was decided on, and for some reason or other "Cinderella" found more favour than any other pantomime idea.

Gwen and Maureen immediately had visions of themselves as perfect Cinderellas, loose hair and all. Maureen turned to Gwen.

52

"How I'd love to act Cinderella," she murmured. "At my last school I . . . "

"Let's see now – what was your last school?" asked Belinda at once.

Poor Maureen didn't dare to say the name. She turned her back on Belinda. "At my last school I was once Cinderella," she said. "I was a great success. I . . . "

Gwen didn't like this kind of thing at all. She began to think Maureen very boring and conceited. Why, *she* had been about to say what a good Cinderella *she* would make! She didn't consider that Maureen, with her weak, silly, rabbit-mouthed face would make a good leading lady at all.

"We'll choose Cinderella for our pantomime story then," said Moira. "We will write the whole thing ourselves. Darrell, you're good at essays – you can draft it out."

Darrell looked enormously surprised. "Draft it out – draft out a whole *pantomime*!" she exclaimed. "Oh, I couldn't. I wouldn't know how to begin."

"You've only got to get the script of one or two other pantomimes to see how to set about it," said Moira. "Can you write verse – and words for songs? We'll have to have those, too."

Darrell wished fervently she wasn't on the committee at all. Why, this was going to be Real Hard Work – just as she thought she was going to have a nice slack term, too. She opened her mouth to protest, but Moira had already finished with her. She was now speaking to Irene.

"Can you get on with the music as soon as we've got the words?" she asked. "Or perhaps you prefer to write the music before you get the words and have them fitted afterwards?"

"I'll work in my own way, thank you," said Irene,

perfectly politely, but with a steady ring in her voice that said, "Keep off! Where music is concerned I'm going to do as I like." She looked straight at Moira. "You can safely leave it to me. Music's my job, it always has been and it always will be."

"Yes, but I must know how you're going to set about it – what kind of tunes you'll write, and so on," said Moira, impatiently. "We can't leave things like that in the air."

"You'll have to as far as I'm concerned," said Irene. "I don't know what tunes I'm going to write till I hear them in my head. Then I'll catch them and write them down. And I don't know *when* I'll hear them either, so don't tell me to sit down at ten each morning and listen for them!"

Catherine tried to pour oil on troubled waters once more. She loved doing that. "Well, after all – when you're dealing with a *genius*," she began. "You can't make rules for geniuses, can you? Moira doesn't quite *understand*, Irene."

"Don't apologize for anything *I* say," said Moira, scowling at Catherine. "What do you mean – I don't quite *understand*! I've done this kind of thing often enough. Didn't I run the show last year, and help to run it the year before that?"

Catherine put on a saintly expression. "Yes, of course, Moira. Don't put yourself out. I shouldn't have said a *word*! I'm sure Irene understands?"

She gave Irene such a sweet smile that everyone felt quite sick. *Did* Catherine have to make herself quite so humble?

The meeting had to come to an abrupt end because the supper bell went. "Good gracious – how the time flew!" said Maureen.

"And now we shan't have time to go to the stables," mourned Bill, dismally.

"We'll call a short committee meeting tomorrow, same time," said Moira, gathering up her things. "We'll tie up any loose ends then."

She swept efficiently out of the room, almost as if she were a mistress!

"Gosh! We'll have to mind our Ps and Qs now," said Daphne, with a comical look. "What *have* we done to have Moira wished on us this term!"

The Balloon Trick

The first week of term always went very slowly indeed. The next week slipped away faster, and then the weeks began to fly. But now it was still only the first week, with a lot of planning and timetables to make, and settling in to be done.

Darrell found herself very busy indeed. She had to attend committee meetings for the Christmas entertainment. She had to read through two or three pantomime scripts, and decide how to draft out her own version of "Cinderella". She found Sally an enormous help here, and discovered that two heads are decidedly better than one.

She was also in charge of the games, and had to draw up practice times for the lower school, and to do a little coaching to help the games mistresses. They consulted with her as to the best players to pick out for matches in the lower school, and Darrell enjoyed feeling important enough to argue with them about the various girls.

"But you *can't* have Rita," she would say. "I know she's good – but she simply won't turn out for practice. She'll go to pieces in a match."

"Well, what do you think of Christine then?" the games mistress would say. "She's so small, I don't like to pick her."

"But she runs like the wind!" Darrell would reply. "And she's so keen. She's just waiting for a chance!"

Yes, Darrell had a lot to do, and she was always busy and always interested in her jobs. The lower school adored her, and vied to win an approving word from her. Felicity was very proud of her fifth-form sister.

"Everyone thinks you're super," she told Darrell. "You should see the way they turn out for practice now – on even the most disgusting days! I say – *have* I got a chance to get into one of the match teams some day, Darrell? You might tell me."

"I can only say that if you go on as you are doing you won't be able to *help* getting in," said Darrell, and Felicity gave a whoop of joy.

June was passing and gave her a sour look. She spoke to Gwyneth, the girl with her. "Talk about favouritism! You'll see Darrell choosing her young sister before anyone else and putting her into the team."

Darrell heard and was over beside June at once. "June! How *dare* you say a thing like that about a fifth-former! Just you wait a minute!"

She fished out the Punishment Book that all the fifth-formers were allowed to have and wrote down June's name in it. She wrote something beside it, tore it out and gave it to June.

"There you are – a little hard work will keep you quiet, and teach you to guard that nasty tongue of yours!"

June took the paper sulkily. She glanced at it. Darrell had written:

"Learn three sonnets of Shakespeare's, and say

56

them to me or one of the other fifth-formers before Tuesday."

She went off with Felicity. "June's awful," remarked Felicity. "If only she wasn't so frightfully funny sometimes, I honestly would never speak to her. Nor would Susan. But she plays such idiotic tricks. She's playing one tomorrow on Mam'zelle Dupont."

"What is it?" asked Darrell, with interest. "I shouldn't have thought there were any tricks left to play on poor old Mam'zelle."

"Well, there are – and June plays them," said Felicity. "And when I see Mam'zelle's face I laugh till I cry."

"Yes, I know – I've laughed till I've ached too, sometimes," said Darrell, remembering some of the jokes she and her form had played at times. "What's June playing at tomorrow?"

"Oh, Darrell," said Felicity, beginning to giggle as she thought of it. "She's got a kind of flat balloon arrangement – well, she's got four, in fact. And you put one under your blouse at the back and another in your front, and another under your skirt at the back, and the last one in front."

Darrell chuckled. "Go on. I can guess what happens."

"Well, June showed us," said Felicity, beginning to laugh helplessly. "All the balloons are joined together by little tubes – and there's an inflator you press to fill them and a deflator you pull out to empty them. When she pressed the inflator she swelled up, you see, and she looked simply *frightful*. Oh, dear – I laughed so much I couldn't sit in my chair."

Darrell laughed, too. "Well, that's a new trick, certainly! I wish we'd had it when *we* were in the first form. Where does June get these tricks from? Alicia always got them from her brothers."

"Oh, June gets advertisement booklets sent her from the firms that make conjuring tricks and funny tricks," said Felicity. "I think she must spend all her pocket money on them."

"It wouldn't be a bad idea to have a spot of conjuring in our pantomime," said Darrell, thoughtfully. "Alicia is awfully good at conjuring. Yes – I'll put a conjurer into the pantomime – it shall be Alicia! If you can borrow that book – or however many she's got – from June, I'd like to look through them."

"Right. But I won't tell her *you* want it," said Felicity. "You'll be mud to her now, after giving her those sonnets to learn. June's doing the trick tomorrow morning at twelve in French Dictée, Darrell. You're not free by any chance, are you? If so, couldn't you come along with some message for Mam'zelle, or something, and see June swell up? You'll know when it's happening because I expect we'll shriek with laughter."

Darrell pondered. She had put that period aside to get on with the draft of the pantomime. Until she had worked out the characters they could not be chosen, so it was important to get on with it. But how could she resist the chance of slipping down to see Mam'zelle's face?

"Well, I'll come if I can," she promised.

But when twelve o'clock came next morning Darrell was called to talk to Matron about some missing socks. Matron always went into matters of this sort very thoroughly indeed, and it was twenty minutes before Darrell was free.

"I wonder what's happened down in the first form?" she thought, feeling rather guilty at her interest in something such babies did. "I wonder if the trick's been played?"

It had. June, who always had to sit in one of the front desks, so as to be under every mistress's eye, had inflated herself very successfully indeed. She did it gradually, so that when Mam'zelle kept looking at her to see that she was getting on with the dictation, she did not at first notice anything.

However, she certainly began to seem a little on the plump side after a bit. Mam'zelle pondered over it. "That child, June – she gets fat. Maybe a little fat will do her good. She is too restless – a truly difficult girl. Now, *fat* girls are not usually difficult – an interesting point."

She glanced at June again and got rather a shock. Why, the child was positively bloated! She stared at June fixedly. One or two of the girls felt such a desire to laugh that it was agony to keep their faces straight. June wrote steadily on. "June!" said Mam'zelle, sharply. "Are you holding your breath?"

June looked innocently at Mam'zelle. "Holding my breath?" she said, with wide eyes. "No. Why should I? But I will if you want me to, Mam'zelle. I can hold it for a long time."

She blew out her cheeks and held her breath. The inflator worked marvellously. She swelled visibly, and Mam'zelle stared in alarm.

"No, no – let out your breath, June. You will burst. What is happening to you?"

June let out her breath with a loud hissing noise, and at the same time pulled the deflator. She deflated at once – and it looked exactly as if it was because she had let out her breath. Mam'zelle was most relieved to see her become her right size again.

"It was rather nice, holding my breath like that," said June, foreseeing a very nice little game of holding her breath and inflating herself, and letting it out and deflating at the same time.

To Mam'zelle's horror she breathed in again, blew out her cheeks and held her breath – and visibly, before Mam'zelle's alarmed gaze, she inflated till she looked really monstrous. Mam'zelle started up from her seat.

"Never have I seen such a thing!" she said, wildly. "June, *je te prie* – I beg you, do not hold your breath in this manner. You will burst."

The whole class burst at that moment. It was impossible to hold their laughter in any longer. June let out her breath and deflated rapidly.

"Don't, don't, June!" gasped Felicity, rolling about in her chair. "Oh don't do it again."

But June did, and Mam'zelle watched wildly whilst she swelled up once more. "Monstrous!" she cried. "June, I beg of you once more. Do not hold your breath again. See how it swells you up, poor child."

And then something went wrong with the deflator! It wouldn't work. June pulled it frantically, but it wouldn't deflate the fat balloons under her clothes. She sat there, pulling wildly at the string fastened to the deflator. It came off!

Mam'zelle was almost in tears. "This poor June! Children, children, how can you laugh? It is no laughing matter. I go, to get help. Matron must come. Be still, June. Do not burst."

She hurried out, wringing her hands. June looked decidedly alarmed. "I say! The beastly thing's gone wrong. I can't let Matron see me like this. I'd get an awful wigging. What can I do?"

Darrell had just arrived at the door at the moment that Mam'zelle rushed out, looking frantic. She had pushed by Darrell without even seeing her. Darrell looked in at the open door.

She saw the monstrous June. Felicity saw Darrell as an angel in disguise. "Darrell! The deflator's gone wrong! Mam'zelle's gone to get Matron. Quick, what can we do?"

"Get a pin, idiot," said Darrell. "Stick it into June and she'll go pop and subside. Then you'd better get her out of that arrangement quickly, because Matron will certainly do some exploring."

A pin was produced. Felicity dug it into the four swellings and they each went off with a loud Pop! June became her own size and shape at once. She began to pull everything out, frantically and wildly. She was frightened now.

She got the rubber balloons out at last and put them into her desk, just as footsteps were heard down the corridor. Darrell slipped out, finding it difficult not to dissolve into laughter. How she would have loved to see Mam'zelle's face when she first saw June swelling up!

Mam'zelle was alone, looking rather subdued. She hurried by Darrell and came to the first form. She went in and gazed at June.

"Ah – so – you are flat now! I told Matron about you and she laughed at me. She said it was a treek. A TREEK! What is this awful, horrible, *abominable* treek? I will find it. I will seek it. I will hunt for it in every desk in the room. Ahhhhhhhh!"

Mam'zelle looked so fierce as she stood there that nobody dared to say a word. June began to wish she had left the balloons in her clothes. If Mam'zelle did look in her desk she would certainly find them.

Mam'zelle found them. She lifted up the lid and saw the rubber balloons at once, flat and torn. She picked them out and shook them in June's face. "Ah, now you can hold your breath again, you bad, wicked June! Hold your breath and listen to what I have to

61

say! You will learn for me one hundred lines of French poetry before Tuesday. Yes, one hundred lines! Does that make you hold your breath, you bad girl?"

It certainly did. June already had two lots of English lines to learn – now she had a hundred French ones to add to the lot. She groaned.

Mam'zelle rummaged further in the desk. She took out some booklets and looked at them.

"New treeks. Old treeks. Treeks to play on your friends. Treeks to play on your enemies," she read. "Aha! These I will take from you, June. You shall do no more treeks this term. These I will confiscate, and I do not think you shall have them back. No!"

She put the booklets with her books on the desk, and, very grim and determined, went on with the French Dictée. The class soon recovered and longed for the last bell to go, so that they might laugh once again to their heart's content.

Mam'zelle said a sharp good morning when the bell went, and went off with the rubber balloons, the booklets about tricks, and her own books. She sat down in the room she shared with Miss Potts, the house mistress of North Tower.

"You look hot and bothered, Mam'zelle," said Miss Potts, sympathetically.

"Ah – this June – she swells up like a frog – under my eyes!" began Mam'zelle, fiercely, swelling up too. Then she saw Miss Potts' astonished look, and smiled suddenly. She opened her mouth and laughed. She rolled in her seat and roared.

"Oh, these treeks! One of these days I too will play a treek. It shall be *superbe, magnifique, merveilleuse*. Ha, one day I too will play a treek!"

In the Common Room

Darrell told Alicia about June's idiotic trick. Alicia laughed. "It's in the family, isn't it! I and my brothers are trick-mad, and now June, my cousin, is going the same way. It's a pity we're in the fifth. I feel it wouldn't be very dignified to play any of our tricks now."

Darrell sighed. "Yes, I suppose you're right. Growing up has its drawbacks, and that's one of them. We have to be dignified and give up some of our silly ideas – but oh, Alicia, I *wish* you could have seen June all blown up – honestly it was as good as any of *your* tricks!"

"It's a pity that cousin of mine is such a hard and brazen little wretch," said Alicia. "I don't actually feel she's afraid of *anything* – except perhaps my brother Sam. The odd thing is she simply adores him, though he's given her some first-class spankings, and won't stand a scrap of nonsense from her when she comes to stay."

"You can't seem to *get* at her, somehow," said Darrell. "I mean – she doesn't seem to care. Well – she's a bit like you, you know, Alicia – though you're a lot better now!"

Alicia went rather pink. "All right. Don't rub it in. I know I'm hard, but you won't make me any better by telling me! You've probably not noticed it but I *have* tried to be more sympathetic with fools and donkeys! Of course, not being either yourself you've had no chance of seeing it."

Darrell laughed. She slipped her arm through Alicia's. "You're a bit of a donkey yourself," she said. "But there's one thing about you that sticks out a mile – and that is your absolute straightness – and I don't feel that about June. Do you? I feel it about my sister Felicity – you could trust her anywhere at any time – but not June. There's something sly about her as well as hard."

"Well, we'll have to lick her into shape whilst we're still at Malory Towers," said Alicia. "We've got two more years to do it in – and then off we go to college – leaving kids like June and Felicity behind to carry on!"

June arrived in the fifth-form common room on Tuesday evening to say her lines to Alicia and Darrell. She looked very sulky. The girls, who were most of them busy with odd jobs such as darning, making out lists, re-writing work, writing letters home and so on, looked up as June strode into the room.

"Don't you know that a lower school kid knocks before she comes in?" said Moira.

June said nothing, but glowered.

"Go out, knock and wait till you're told to come in," ordered Moira, in her dictatorial voice. June hesitated. She detested being ordered about.

Moira felt in her pocket for her little Punishment Book, and June fled. She didn't want any more lines!

"I never knew anyone who so badly needed licking into shape," said Moira, grimly. "Little toad! I know she's your cousin, Alicia, but she's no credit to you!"

"I can't say your sister Bridget is much credit to *you* either," retorted Alicia. She didn't particularly want to defend June, but she resented Moira's high and mighty manner. Let her look after her own bad-mannered cousin!

"June's knocked twice already," said Catherine. "Oughtn't we to say 'come in'?"

"When I say so," said Moira. "Do her good to wait."

June knocked again. "Come in," said Moira, and June came in, red and furious. She went to Darrell and silently gave her the book out of which she had learnt her lines.

"Repeat them to me," said Darrell. June gabbled them off without a single mistake. Darrell looked at her. She really was very like Alicia – and she had Alicia's marvellous memory, too. No doubt it had taken June only about five minutes to memorize that long poem.

She went to Alicia, and gabbled off what she had learnt for her, again with no mistake. "Right," said Alicia. "You can go – and if you don't want to spend the whole of this term learning lines, try to be more civil to your elders."

June scowled. Belinda whipped out her pencil.

"Hold it!" she said to the surprised June. "Yes – just like that – mouth down, brows frowning, surly expression. Hold it, hold it! I want it for my Scowl Book. It's called 'How to Scowl', and it's really interesting. You should see some of the scowls I've got!"

Moira and Gwendoline, who knew they had contributed to this unique book, immediately scowled with annoyance, and then straightened their faces at once in case Belinda saw them. Blow Belinda! One couldn't even scowl in peace with her around.

June stood still, scowling even more fiercely. "Done?" she said at last. "Well, I wish you joy of all your scowls – I'll be willing to come along and offer you a good selection any time you like. It's an easy thing to do when any fifth-former is around."

She stalked off, feeling in her pocket for the lines she had learnt for Mam'zelle. They hadn't really taken her very long. Thank goodness for a parrot memory! June had only to read lines through once, saying them out loud, to know them. Others with less good memories envied her tremendously. It didn't seem fair that June, who tried so little, could do such good work, and that they, who tried so hard, very often only produced bad or ordinary work!

"Blow!" said Irene, suddenly, putting down her pencil. She had been composing a little galloping tune, the one that had been in her head for some time after she had heard the galloping hooves of the horses in the drive. "I'm just nicely in the middle of this tirretty-too tune – and I've just remembered it's my turn to do the flowers in the classroom. I ought to go and pick them before it's quite dark."

"Let *me* go," said Catherine, putting down her darning. "I'll be pleased to do it for you. You're *such* a genius, Irene – you just go on with your tune. I'm only an ordinary mortal – no gifts at all – and it's a pleasure to do what little I can."

She smiled her beaming smile, and Irene felt slightly sick. Everyone was getting tired of Catherine and her martyr-like ways. She was always putting herself out for someone, offering to do the jobs nobody else wanted to do, belittling herself, and praising others extravagantly.

"No, thanks," said Irene, shortly. "It's my job and I must do it."

"How like you to feel like that!" gushed Catherine.

"Well – I'm quite busy darning Gwendoline's stocking, so if you *really* wouldn't like me to do the flowers for you, I'll . . . "

But Irene was gone. She slammed the door and nobody except Catherine minded. They all felt like slamming the door themselves.

"I do think Irene might have said thank you,"

said Catherine, in rather a hurt voice. "Don't you, Maureen?"

Maureen felt that everyone was waiting to pounce on her if she dared to say "yes". Irene was so very popular. She was hesitating about how to answer when the door opened and Irene came back.

"Someone's done the flowers!" she said.

"Yes – now I come to think of it, I saw Clarissa doing them," said Mavis.

"What on earth for?" demanded Irene. "Gosh – I hope people aren't going to run round after me doing my jobs! I'm still perfectly capable of doing them."

"Well," said Darrell, suddenly remembering, "it's Clarissa's week, idiot. Your week is next week. You looked it up this morning."

"Gosh!" said Irene again, with a comical air of dismay. "I'm nuts! I go and interrupt my own bit of composing, and rush off to do a job I'm not supposed to do till next week. Anyway – it gave dear Catherine a chance to make one of her generous offers!"

"That's not kind of you, Irene," said Catherine, flushing "But never mind – I do understand. If I could compose like you I'd say nasty things sometimes, I expect! I do understand."

"Could you stop being forgiving and understanding long enough for me to finish my tune?" said Irene, in a dangerous voice. "I don't care if you 'understand' or not – all I care about at the moment is to finish this."

Catherine put on a saintly face, pressed her lips together as if stopping herself from retorting, and went on darning.

There was a knock at the door. Irene groaned. "Go away! Don't come in!"

The door opened and Connie's face peered round. "Is Ruth here? Ruth, can you come for a minute? Bridget is out here. We've got rather a good idea."

"I don't like Bridget," said Ruth, in a low voice. "And anyway I'm busy. So's everyone else here."

"But, Ruth – I've hardly seen you this week," protested Connie. "Come on out for a minute. By the way, I've mended your roller skates for you. They're ready for you to use again."

Irene groaned. Darrell groaned too. She was trying to draft out the third act of the pantomime.

"Either tell Connie to go, or go yourself," said Irene. "If not, *I'll* go! I'll go and sit in the bathroom and take this with me. Perhaps I'll get a few minutes peace then. Tirretty-tirretty-too. Yes, I think I'll go."

She got up. Connie fled, thinking Irene was going to row her. Ruth looked round apologetically, but said nothing.

"It's all right," said Darrell, softly. "Keep Connie at arm's length till she leaves you in peace, Ruth – and don't worry about it!"

But Catherine had to be silly about it, of course. "Poor Connie," she said. "I really can't help feeling sorry for her. We oughtn't to be *too* bad on her, ought we?"

The Weeks Go On

Now the days began to slip by more quickly. Two weeks went – three weeks – and then the fourth week turned up and began to slip away, too.

Everything was going well. There was no illness in the school. The weather was fine, so that the playing-fields were in use every day, and there was plenty of practice for everyone. Work was going well, and except for the real duds, nobody was doing badly. Five lacrosse matches had already been won by the school, and Darrell, as games captain for the fifth, was in the seventh heaven of delight.

She had played in two of the matches, and had shot both the winning goals. Felicity had gone nearly mad with joy. She had been able to watch Darrell in both because they were home matches. Felicity redoubled her practices and begged Darrell for all the coaching time she could spare. She was reserve for the fourth school team, and was determined to be in it before the end of the term.

The plans for the Christmas entertainment were going well, too. So far no help had been asked from either Mr Young, the music teacher, or Miss Greening, the elocution mistress. The girls had planned everything themselves.

Darrell had been amazed at the way she and Sally had been able to grasp the planning of a big panto-mime. At first it had seemed a hopeless task, and Darrell hadn't had the faintest idea how to set about it. But now, having got down to it with Sally, having read up a few other plays and pantomimes, and got the general idea, she was finding that she seemed to have quite a gift for working out a new one!

"It's wonderful!" she said to Sally. "I didn't know I *could*. I'm loving it. I say, Sally – do you think, do you *possibly* think I might have a sort of gift that way? I never thought I had any gift at all."

"Yes," said Sally, loyally. "I think you *have* got a gift for this kind of thing. That's the best of a school like this, that has so many many interests – there's something for everybody – and if you *have* got a hidden or sleeping gift you're likely to find it, and be able to use it. There's your way of scribbling down verse, too – I never knew you could do that before!"

"Nor did I, really," said Darrell. She fished among her papers and pulled out a scribbled sheet. "Can I read you this, Sally? It's the song Cinderella is supposed to sing as she sits by the fire, alone. Her sisters have gone to the ball. Listen:

"By the fire I sit and dream
And in the flames I see,
Pictures of the lovely things
That never come to me,
That never come to me,
Ah me!

Carriages, a lovely gown,
A flowing silver cloak –
The embers move, the picture's gone,
My dreams go up in smoke,
My dreams go up in smoke,
In smoke!"

She stopped. "That's as far as I've got with that song. Of course, I know it's not awfully good, and certainly not poetry, only just verse – but I never in my life knew I could even put things in rhyme! And, of course, Irene just gobbles them up, and sets them to delicious tunes in no time."

"Yes. It's very good," said Sally. "You do enjoy it all, too, don't you? I say – what *will* your parents think when they come to the pantomime and see on the programme that Darrell Rivers has written the words – and the songs, too!"

"I don't know. I don't think they'll believe it," said Darrell.

Darrell was not the only member of the fifth form enjoying herself over the production of the pantomime. Irene was too – she was setting Darrell's songs

71

to exactly the right tunes, and scribbling down the harmonies as if she had been composing all her life long – as she very nearly had, for Irene was humming melodies before she was one year old!

The class were used to seeing Irene coming along the corridor or up the stairs, bumping unseeingly into them, humming a new tune. "Tumty-ta, ti-ta, ti-ta, tumty-too. Oh, sorry, Mavis. I honestly didn't see you. Tumty-ta, ti-ta – gosh, did I hurt you, Catherine. I never saw you coming."

"Oh, that's *quite* all right," said Catherine, gently patting Irene on the arm, and making her shy away at once. "We don't have geniuses like you every . . ."

But Irene was gone. How she detested Catherine with her humble ways, and her continual air of sacrificing herself for others!

"Tumty-ta, ti-ta," she hummed suddenly in class, and banged her hand down on the desk. "Got it! Of course, that's it! Oh, *sorry*, Miss Jimmy – er, James, I mean, Miss James. I just got carried away for a moment. I've been haunted by . . ."

"You needn't explain," said Miss James, with a twinkle in her eye. "Do you think you've got that particular tune out of your system now, and could concentrate, say, for half an hour, on what the rest of the class are doing?"

"Oh yes – yes, of course," said Irene, still rather bemused. She bent over her maths book, pencil in hand. Miss James was amused to see one page of figures and one page of scribbled music, when the book was given in – both excellent, for Irene was almost as much a genius at maths as at music. She insisted that the two things went together, though this seemed unbelievable to the rest of the class. Maths were so dull and music so lovely!

The words of the pantomime progressed fast, and so

did the music. It was essential that they should because there could be no rehearsing until there was something to rehearse!

Belinda was busy with designs for scenery and costumes. She, too, was extremely happy. Her pencil flew over the paper each evening and every moment of free time – she drew everything, even the pattern on Cinderella's apron!

Little Janet waited eagerly as the designs grew and were passed on to her. She too was eager and enthusiastic. She turned out the enormous trunks of dresses and tunics and costumes of all periods, used by other girls at Malory Towers in terms gone by. How could she alter this? How could she use that? Oh, what a wonderful piece of blue velvet! Just right for the Prince!

Little Janet had always been ingenious, but now she surpassed herself. She chose out all the material and stuffs she needed, with unerring taste – she sorted out dresses and costumes that could be altered. She ran round the school pressing all the good needleworkers into her service. She begged Miss Linnie, the quiet little sewing mistress, to help her by allowing some of the classes to work on the clothes and decorations.

"I would never have thought that little mouse of a Janet had it in her to blossom out like this!" said Miss Potts to Mam'zelle. "What these children can do if they're just given a chance to do things on their own!"

Another person who was working hard, though in quite a different direction, was Alicia! Alicia, who never worked really hard at anything, because she had good brains and didn't need to. But now she had something to do that, brains or no brains, needed constant hard work and practice.

Alicia was to be the Demon King in the pantomime

– and he was to be an enchanter, a conjurer who could do magic things! Alicia was to show her skill at conjuring, and she meant to be as good a conjurer on the school stage as any conjurer in a London pantomime.

"Well – I didn't dream that Alicia's ability for playing silly tricks and doing bits of amateur conjuring to amuse her friends would make her work as hard as *this*," said Miss Peters, the third-form mistress, shutting the door of one of the music-rooms softly.

She had heard peculiar sounds in there – sounds of pantings, sounds of something falling, sounds of sheer exasperation, and she had peeped in to see what in the world was going on.

Alicia was there, with her back to her, practising a spot of juggling! Yes, she was going to juggle, as well as conjure – and she had an array of coloured rings which she was throwing rapidly up into the air, one after another, catching them miraculously.

Then she would miss one, and click in exasperation. She would have to begin all over again. Ah – Alicia had found something that didn't need only brainwork – it needed patience, practice, deftness, and then patience all over again.

"Why did I ever say I'd be the Demon King!" groaned Alicia, picking up the rings for the twenty-second time and beginning again. "Why did I ever agree to do conjuring and juggling? I must have been mad."

But her pride made her go on and on. If Alicia did a thing it had to be done better than anybody else could possibly do it. The fifth form were most intrigued by this new interest of Alicia's. It was such fun to see her suddenly pick up a pencil, rubber, ruler and pen, and juggle them rapidly in the air, catching them deftly in one hand at the finish!

It was amusing to see her get up to find Mam'zelle's

fountain pen, and pick it apparently out of the empty air, and even more amusing to see her gravely abstract an egg from Mam'zelle's ear.

"Alicia! I will not have such a thing!" stormed Mam'zelle. "Oh, *là là*! Now you have found a cigarette in my other ear. It is not nice! It makes me go – what do you call it – duck-flesh."

"Goose-flesh, Mam'zelle," said Alicia, with one of her wicked grins. "Dear me – has your fountain pen gone again? It's up in the air as usual!" And she reached out her hand and picked it once more from the air.

No wonder the class liked Alicia's new interest. It certainly added a lot more enjoyment to lessons!

Gwendoline Mary and Maureen

Two girls were anxiously waiting for Darrell to finish the pantomime. They were Gwendoline and Maureen. Each of them saw herself in the part of Cinderella. Each of them crept away in the dormy on occasion, let her golden hair loose, and posed in front of the dressing-table mirrors.

"I look exactly right for Cinderella," thought Gwendoline Mary. "I'm the *type*, somehow. I could sit pensively by the fireside and look really lovely. And as the princess at the ball I'd be wonderful."

She wrote and told her mother about the coming pantomime. "Of course, we don't know *yet* about the characters," she said. "Most of the girls would like me to be Cinderella – they say I *look* the part. I don't know what *you* think, Mother? I'm not conceited, as you know, but I can't help thinking I'd do it rather well. What does Miss Winter think?"

Back came two gushing letters at once, one from her delighted mother, one from her old governess, worshipping as ever.

DARLING GWEN,

Yes, of course you must be Cinderella. You would be *absolutely right*. Your hair would look so lovely in the firelight. Oh, how proud I shall be to see you sitting there pensive and sad, looking into . . .

And so on and so on. Miss Winter's letter was much the same. Both of them had apparently taken it completely for granted that Gwendoline would have the chief part.

Moira came barging into the dormy one day and discovered a startled Gwendoline standing in front of her mirror, her hair all round her face, and a towel thrown over her shoulders for an evening cloak.

"Gosh – what *do* you think you're doing?" she said, in amazement. "Washing your hair or something? Are you mad, Gwen? You can't wash your hair at this time of day. You're due for French in five minutes."

Gwendoline muttered something and flung the towel back on its rack. She went bright red. Moira was puzzled.

Two days later Moira again came rushing into the dormy to see if the windows were open. This time she found Maureen standing in front of *her* mirror, her hair loose down her back in a golden sheet, and one of the cubicle curtains pinned round her waist to make a train.

Moira gaped. Maureen went pink and began to brush her hair as if it was a perfectly ordinary thing to be found with it loose, and a curtain pinned to her waist.

Moira found her voice. "What do you and Gwen think you're doing, parading about here with your hair loose and towels and curtains draped round you?" she demanded. "Have you both gone crackers? Every time I come into this dormy I see you or Gwen with your hair loose and things draped round you. What are you up to?"

Maureen couldn't possibly tell the scornful practical Moira what she was doing – merely pretending to be a beautiful Cinderella with a cloud of glorious hair and a long golden train to her dress. But Moira suddenly guessed.

She laughed her loud and scornful laugh. "Oh! I believe *I* know! You're playing Cinderella! Both of you pretending to be Cinderella. What a hope you've got! We'd never choose Rabbit-Teeth to play Cinderella."

And with this very cutting remark Moira went out of the room, laughing loudly. Maureen gazed at herself in the mirror and tears came to her eyes. Rabbit-Teeth! How *horrible* of Moira. How frightfully cruel. She couldn't help her teeth being like that. Or could she? Very guiltily Maureen remembered how she had been told to wear a wire round her front teeth to force them back – and she hadn't been able to get used to it, and had tucked it away in her drawer at Mazeley Manor.

Nobody there had said anything about it. Nobody had bothered. Mazeley Manor was a free and easy school, as Maureen was so fond of saying, comparing it unfavourably with Malory Towers, and its compulsory games, its inquisitive Matron and determined, responsible house mistresses.

"If I'd been *here* when the dentist told me to wear that wire round my teeth, Matron and Miss Potts would both have made me do it, even if I didn't want to," she thought. "And by now I'd have nice teeth – not sticking-out and ugly."

And for the first time a doubt about that wonderful school, Mazeley Manor, crept into Maureen's mind. Was it so good after all to be allowed to do just as you liked? To play games or not as you liked? To go for walks or not at your own choice? Perhaps – yes, perhaps it *was* better to *have* to do things that were good for you, whether you liked them or not, till you were old enough and responsible enough to choose.

Maureen had chosen not to wear the wire when she should have done – and now she had been called Rabbit-Teeth, and she was sure she wouldn't be chosen as Cinderella. She did up her hair rather soberly, blinking away a few more tears, and trying to shut her lips over the protruding front teeth.

She forgot to unpin the curtain, and went out of the room, thinking so deeply that she didn't even feel it dragging behind her. She met Mam'zelle at the top of the stairs.

"*Tiens!*" said Mam'zelle, stopping in surprise. "*Que fais-tu*, Maureen? What are you doing with that curtain?"

Maureen cast a horrified look at her "train" and rushed back to the dormy. She unpinned it and put the curtain back into its place. Feeling rather subdued she went downstairs to find Gwen.

Gwen was getting very very tired of Maureen. The new girl had fastened onto her like a leech. She related long and boring stories of her parents, her friends, her old school and especially of herself. She never seemed to think that Gwen would like to talk too.

Gwen sometimes broke into the middle of Maureen's boring speeches. "Maureen, did I ever tell you about the time I went to Norway? My word, it was super. I stayed up to dinner each night, and I was only thirteen, and . . ."

"I've never been to Norway," Maureen would interrupt. "But my aunt went there last summer. She sent me a whole lot of postcards. I'll find them to show you. You'll be interested to see them, I'm sure."

Gwen wasn't interested. She was never interested in anything anyone else ever showed her. In fact, like Maureen, she wasn't interested in anything except herself.

The only time that Maureen ever really listened to her was when she told unkind tales of the others in the form. Then Maureen would listen with great interest. "I wouldn't have thought it of Darrell," she would say. "Good gracious, did Daphne really do that? Oh, I say – fancy *Bill* being so deceitful!"

Gwen was forced to play games and not only that but to take part in a lot of practices. She was made to do gym properly, and never allowed to get out of it by announcing she didn't feel too well. She had to go for every walk that was planned, fuming and furious.

It was June who enlightened Maureen about all this assiduous attendance at games, gym and walks. She told her gleefully the history of Gwen's weak heart the term before.

"Gwen wanted to get out of the School Cert. exam, so she foxed and said she'd a weak heart that fluttered like a bird!" grinned June. "Her mother took her home. And then it was discovered Gwen was pretending and back she came just in time for the exam – and ever since she's been made to go in for games and gym like anything. She's a humbug!"

June had no right to say all this to a senior, and Maureen had no right to listen to her. But, like Gwen, she loved a bit of spiteful gossip, and she stored the information up in her mind, though she said nothing to Gwen about it.

The two girls were forced to be together a great

deal. Almost everyone else in the form had their own friend. Moira had no particular friend, but went with Catherine, who was always at anyone's disposal. So Gwen and Maureen, being odd ones out, had to walk together, and were left together very often when everyone else was doing something.

Gwen grew to detest Maureen. Horrid, conceited, selfish creature! She hated the sound of her voice. She tried to avoid her when she could. She made excuses not to be with her.

But Maureen wouldn't let her go. Gwen was the only one available to be talked to, and boasted to, and on occasion, when she had fallen foul of Miss James, to be wailed to.

Maureen thought she could draw as well as Belinda – or almost as well. She thought she could sing beautifully – and, indeed, she had an astonishingly powerful voice which, alas, continually went off the true note, and was flat. She was certain she could compose tunes as well as Irene. And she even drove Darrell to distraction by offering to write a few verses for her.

"What are we to do with this pest of a Maureen?" complained Janet, one evening. "She comes and asks if she can help me and then if I give her the simplest thing to sew, she goes and botches it up so that I have to undo it."

"And she had the sauce to come and tell me she didn't like some of my chords in the opening chorus of 'Cinderella'," snorted Irene. "I ticked her off. But she won't *learn* she's not wanted. She won't learn she's no good! She's so thick-skinned that I'm sure a bullet would bounce off her if she was shot!"

"She wants a lesson," said Alicia. "My word – if she comes and offers to show me how to juggle, I'll juggle her! I'll juggle her all down the corridor and

81

back again, and down into the garden and on to the rocks and into the pool!"

"Gwen's looking pretty sick these days," said Belinda. "She doesn't like having a double that clings to her like Maureen does. I wonder if she knows how like her Maureen is. In silliness and boringness and conceitedness and boastfulness and . . . !"

"Oh, I say," said the saintly Catherine, protesting. "Aren't you being rather unkind, Belinda?"

Belinda looked at Catherine. "There are times to be kind and times to be unkind, dear sweet Catherine," she said. "But you don't seem to know them. You think you're being kind to me when you sharpen all my pencils to a pin-point – but you're not. You're just being interfering. I don't *want* all my pencils like that. I keep some of them blunt on purpose. And about this being unkind to Maureen. Sometimes unkindness is a short cut to putting something right. I guess that's what Maureen wants – a dose of good hard common-sense administered sharply. And that's what she'll get if she doesn't stop this silly nonsense of hers."

Catherine put on her martyr-like air. "You know best, of course, Belinda. I wouldn't dream of disagreeing with you. I'm sorry about the pencils. I just go round seeing what I can do to help, that's all."

"Shall I show you how you look in your own thoughts, Catherine?" said Belinda, suddenly. Everyone listened, most amused at Belinda's sudden outburst. She was usually so very good-natured – but people like Maureen, Gwen and Catherine could be very very trying.

Belinda's pencil flew over a big sheet of paper. She worked at it for five minutes, then took up a pin. "I'll pin it to the wall, girls," she said. "Catherine will simply *love* it. It's the living image of her as she imagines herself."

She took the sheet to the wall and pinned it up. The girls crowded round. Catherine, consumed with curiosity, went too.

It was a picture of her standing in a stained-glass window, a gleaming halo round her head. Underneath, in big bold letters Belinda had written five words:

OUR BLESSED MARTYR, ST CATHERINE

Catherine fled away from the shrieks of delighted laughter. "She's got what she wanted!" said Darrell. "Catherine, come back! How do you like being a saint in a stained-glass window?"

A Plot – and a Quarrel

Before that week had ended Darrell was ready with the whole pantomime, words and all. Most of the music had been written, because Irene almost snatched the words from Darrell as she finished them.

"Quite a Gilbert and Sullivan," said Moira, rather sneeringly, speaking of the famous comic opera pair of the last century. She was feeling rather out of things. Until the pantomime was written, she could not produce it, so she had nothing to do at the moment. And Moira disliked having nothing to do. She liked running things, organizing things and people, dominating everyone, laying down the law.

She was not a popular head girl. The fifth-formers resented her dictatorial manner. They disliked her lack of humour, and they took as little notice of her as they could.

Moira chafed under all this. "Do buck up with this pantomime, Darrell and Sally," she said. "I wish I'd undertaken to write it myself now, you're so slow."

"You *couldn't* write it," said Darrell. "You know you couldn't. You hardly ever get good marks for composition."

Moira flushed. "Don't be cheeky," she said.

Catherine spoke up for her, using a sweet and gentle voice. "I'm sure Moira only let you and Sally do it to give you a chance," she said. "I'm sure she could have done it very well herself."

"There speaks our blessed martyr, Saint Catherine," put in Alicia, maliciously. "Dear Saint Catherine. She deserves the halo Belinda gave her, doesn't she, girls?"

Catherine frowned. Belinda called out at once. "Hold it, Catherine, hold it! No, don't smile in that sickly sweet manner, let me have that frown again!"

Catherine turned away. It was too bad that she should be laughed at when all the time she was trying to be kind and self-sacrificing and really *good*, poor Catherine thought to herself. She glanced at the wall. Blow! There was yet another picture of her up there, with a bigger halo than ever!

Catherine regularly sneaked into the common room when it was empty, and took down the pictures that Belinda as regularly drew of her. But always there was a fresh one. It was absolutely maddening. This one showed her sharpening thousands of pencils, and if anyone looked carefully at the big halo they could see that it, too, was made of sharpened pencils set closely together.

"It's enough to make anyone furiously angry," thought Catherine. "I wonder I don't lose my temper and break out, and call people names. Well – I *try* to like them all, but it's very very difficult."

The fifth form decided they must deal with Maureen

as well as with Catherine. "Better show them both exactly where they stand before we begin rehearsing," said Alicia. "We can't be bothered by interferers and whiners and saints when once we're on the job. Now – how shall we deal with Maureen?"

"The trouble with *her* is that she's so full of herself – thinks she can do everything better than anyone else, and is sure she could run the whole show," said Darrell. "She's so jolly thick-skinned there's no doing anything with her. She's too vain for words!"

"Right," said Alicia. "We'll give her a real chance. We'll tell her to draw some designs to help Belinda – we'll tell her to sing one or two songs to help Mavis. We'll tell her to compose one or two tunes to help Irene – and write one or two poems to help Sally. Then we'll turn the whole lot down scornfully, and she'll know where she stands."

"Well – it sounds rather *drastic*," said Mary-Lou.

"It does, rather," said Sally. "Can't we tell her to do the things – and let her down not *too* scornfully?"

"Yes. We could pretend she wasn't being serious – she was just pulling our legs when she brings the tunes and verses and things," said Darrell. "And we could pat her on the back and clap and laugh – but not take them seriously at all. If she's got any commonsense she'll shut up after that. If she hasn't, we'll have to be a bit more well – *drastic*, as Mary-Lou calls it."

Everyone was in this plot except Gwen and Catherine. The girls were afraid one of the two might tell tales to Maureen if they knew of the plan. Moira approved of it, though she thought it not whole-hearted enough. She would have liked the first idea, the "drastic" one.

Maureen was told to submit verses, tunes and designs. Also to learn two of the songs in case she could improve on Mavis's interpretation of them.

She was so gratified and delighted that she could hardly stammer her thanks. At last she was coming into her own. Her gifts were being recognized! How wonderful!

She rushed straight off to tell Gwen. Gwen could hardly believe her ears. She listened, green with jealousy. To ask *Maureen* to do these things! It was unbelievable.

"Aren't you pleased, Gwen? I can do them all better than the others, can't I?" cried Maureen, her pale blue eyes shining brightly. "At last the others are beginning to realize that I *did* learn something at Mazeley Manor."

"You and your Measley Manor," said Gwen, turning away. Maureen was shocked. Had *Gwen*, Gwen her friend, actually said "Measley"? She must have misheard. She took Gwen by the arm, chattering happily.

But Gwen was strangely unfriendly. She was so jealous that she could hardly answer a word.

Maureen worked hard. She produced two lots of verses, two tunes, and a variety of designs for costumes. She learnt the two songs that Darrell had given her, going alone into a fifth-form music room, where she let her loud voice out to such an extent, and so much off the note, that the girls in the next music rooms listened, startled and amazed.

It was not only a loud voice, but it was not true in pitch – it kept sliding off the note, and going flat, like a gramophone just about to run down. It made the astonished girls in the rooms nearby shiver down their spines. Whoever could it be, yowling like that?

Bridget, Moira's fourth-form sister, went to have a look. Gracious, it was a fifth-former yowling in there – who was it – Maureen Little! Bridget grinned and went to find Connie. The two of them had become friends, and Connie was gradually leaving Ruth to herself, coming less and less to ask for her company.

The two fourth-formers peered into the square of glass set in the door of the practice room where Maureen was singing.

"Hear that?" said Bridget, maliciously. "Wonderful, isn't it? Let's both go into the room next door and yowl too. Come on. It's empty now. If a fifth-former's allowed to do that, so are we!"

So the two of them went next door and made such a hullaballoo, pretending to be a couple of opera-singers, that everyone in the corridor was startled.

Only Maureen, lost in her loud voice, soaring to higher and louder heights, heard nothing. Her door suddenly opened and Moira came in.

"MAUREEN! Shut up! We can even hear you in the common room!"

Maureen stopped abruptly. Then, from the next room rose more yowls. Moira hurried there, amazed. *Now* what was going on?

Connie stopped as soon as she saw Moira. But Bridget, who cared nothing for her sister's anger, sang on vigorously, altering the words of her song at once.

"OHHHHHHH! Here is MOIRA! HERE – is SHEEE."

"Bridget! Stop that at once!" said Moira, angrily. But Bridget didn't stop.

"HERE – is SHEE-EEE!" she repeated.

"Did you hear what I said?" shouted Moira.

Bridget stopped for breath. "I'm not making nearly such a noise as Maureen," she said. "And anyway I keep on the note and she doesn't. If a fifth-former can yowl away like that why can't we?"

"Now don't you start being cheeky," began Moira, going white with annoyance. "You know I won't stand that. Connie, go out of the room. I advise you not to make close friends with Bridget. You'll only get yourself into trouble."

Connie went, scared. If it had been Ruth with her, in trouble, she would have stayed and stuck up for her – but Bridget was different. She always stood up for herself. She faced Moira now.

"*That's* a nice thing to tell anyone about your sister, Moira," she said. "Washing your dirty linen in public! Telling somebody I'm not fit to make friends with."

"I *didn't* say that," said Moira. "Why can't you behave yourself, Bridget? I'm ashamed of you. I'm always hearing things about you."

"Well, so am I about you!" said Bridget. "Who is the most domineering person in the fifth? You! Who is the most unpopular head girl they've ever had? You! Who didn't go up with the old fifth form because nobody could put up with her? You!"

"*Oh!*" cried Moira, whiter still with rage. "You're unbearable. I shall report you to Miss Williams, yes, and Connie too. And I shall report you every single time I find you doing something you shouldn't. *I* know how you sneak out of your dormy at night to talk to the third-formers. *I* know how you get out of the jobs you ought to do. *I* hear things too!"

"Sneak," said Bridget.

It was a very ugly sight, the two sisters standing there, shouting at one another. Moira was trembling now and so was Bridget. Moira had to keep her hands well down to her side, she so badly wanted to strike her sister. Bridget kept well out of the way. She always came off worst in a struggle.

There was a pause. "You'll be sorry if you do report me about this afternoon," said Bridget at last. "Very sorry. I *warn* you. Go and report Maureen! She'll expect it of the domineering Moira! But just

88

remember – I've *warned* you – you'll be sorry if you report *me*."

"Well, I shall," said Moira. "It's my duty to. Fourth-formers aren't allowed in these practice rooms, you know that."

She turned and left the room, still trembling. She went to find Miss Williams, the fourth-form mistress. If she didn't report those two straightaway, whilst she was furious, she might not do it when her anger had died down.

Miss Williams was rather cool about the affair. She wrote down the two fourth-form names Moira gave her, and nodded. "Right. I'll speak to them."

That was all. Moira wished she hadn't said anything. She felt uncomfortable now about Bridget's threats. How could Bridget make her sorry? Bridget was so very fierce sometimes, and did such unaccountable things – like the time when she had broken every single one of Moira's dolls, years ago, because Moira had thrown one of Bridget's toys out of the window.

Yes, Moira felt decidedly uncomfortable as she walked back to the common room. Bridget would certainly get back at her if she could!

The Plot is Successful

Maureen had been rather scared at Moira's sudden arrival in the practice room. She had heard the angry voices in the next room too, when Moira had left her, and had been even more scared. It didn't take much to scare Maureen! She slipped hurriedly out of the room and went off to the classroom to put the finishing touches to her designs. She was to show them to the others that evening.

She saw Gwen's sour face as she walked into the common room with her sheaf of designs, and sheets and sheets of music and verses. Oh, Maureen had been very busy! If Mam'zelle and Miss James had known how hard she had been at work they would have been most surprised. Neither of them had any idea that Maureen had it in her to work at all.

"*What* they taught at Mazely Manor I really do not know," Miss James said to the other teachers each time she corrected Maureen's work.

"Self-admiration – self-esteem – self-pity," murmured Miss Williams, who taught one lesson in the fifth form, and had had quite enough of Maureen.

"But not self-control," said Miss James. "What a school! It's a good thing it's shut down."

Everyone was in the common room waiting for Maureen, though neither Gwen nor Catherine knew the little plot that was being hatched by the rest. Maureen beamed round. "*Now* you're going to see something," she said, gaily, and laughed her silly little laugh. "It was always said at Mazeley Manor that I was a good all-rounder – don't think I'm boasting, will you – but honestly, though I say it myself, I *can* do most things!"

Maureen was surprised to hear some of the girls laughing quite hilariously.

"You're such a *joker*, Maureen," said Alicia, appreciatively. "Always being really humorous."

This was a new idea to Maureen. Nobody had ever called her humorous before. She at once went up in her own estimation.

"Now," she said, "I'll show you the designs first. This is for Cinderella's ball costume – I've gone back to the sixteenth century for it, as you see."

Shrieks of laughter came from everyone. "Priceless!" said Darrell, pretending to wipe her eyes. "How can you think of it, Maureen?"

"A perfect scream," said Mavis, holding up the crude drawing, with its poor colouring. "What a joke! I didn't know you'd such a sense of humour, Maureen."

Maureen was puzzled. She hadn't meant the drawing to be funny at all. She had thought it was beautiful. She hurried on to the next one – but the girls forestalled her and picked up the sheets, showing them round to one another with squeals of laughter.

"Look at this one! I never saw anything so funny in my life!"

"Good enough for *Punch*! I *say* – look at the baron's *face*! And what *is* he wearing?"

"This one's priceless. Gosh, Maureen really is a humorist, isn't she?"

Then Irene picked up the sheets of music. "Hallo! Here are the tunes she has written! I bet they'll be priceless, too. I'll play them over."

She went to the common-room piano, and with a very droll expression on her face she played the tunes, making them sound even sillier than they were.

Everyone crowded round the piano, laughing. "Isn't Maureen a scream! She can do funny drawings and write ridiculous tunes too!"

Maureen began to feel frightened. Were the girls really in earnest about all this? They seemed to be. Surely – surely – they couldn't *really* think that all her lovely work was so bad that it was funny? They must be thinking it was funny on purpose – perhaps they thought she meant it to be!

She turned to find Gwen. Gwen would understand. Gwen was her friend, she had told Gwen everything – how good she was at drawing, music and singing, how hard she had worked at all this, how pleased she was with the results.

Gwen was looking at her and it wasn't a nice look. It was a triumphant look that said, "Ah – pride comes before a fall, my girl – and what a fall!" It was a look that said, "I'm glad about all this. Serves you right."

Maureen was shocked. Gwen laughed loudly, and joined in with the others.

"Frightfully funny! Priceless, Maureen! Who would have thought you could be so funny?"

"Now sing," said Mavis, and thrust one of the songs into her hand. "Let's hear you. You've such a wonderful voice, haven't you, so well trained. I'm sure it must be a great joy to you. Sing!"

Maureen did not dare to refuse. She gazed at the music with blurred eyes and sang. Her loud voice rose even more off the note than usual. It shook with disappointment as the girls began to clap and cheer and laugh again.

"Ha ha! Listen to that! Can't she have a *comic* part in the play, Darrell, and sing it? She'd bring the house down. Did you ever hear such a voice?"

Maureen stopped singing. Tears fell down her cheek. She gave one desperate look at Gwen, a look begging for a word of praise – but none came.

She turned to go out of the room. Catherine ran after her. "Maureen! Don't take it like that. The girls don't *mean* anything!"

"Oh yes we do," said Darrell, under her breath. "We've been cruel to be kind. Catherine *would* say a thing like that."

"Don't touch me!" cried Maureen. "*Saint* Catherine – coming all over pious and goody-goody after you've laughed at me with the rest! Ho – SAINT!"

Catherine shrank back as if she had been slapped in the face. Nobody smiled, except Gwen. Mary-Lou looked upset. She couldn't bear scenes of any sort. Bill looked on stolidly. She got up.

"Well, I'm going riding," she said. "There's half an hour of daylight left. Coming, Clarissa?"

Bill's stolidness and matter-of-fact voice made everyone feel more normal. They watched Bill and Clarissa go out of the room.

"Well – I don't somehow feel that was quite such a success as we hoped," said Sally. "Actually I feel rather low."

"So do I," said Darrell. "Maureen *is* a conceited ass, of course, and badly needed taking down a peg – but I'm afraid we've taken her down more pegs that we meant to."

"It won't hurt her," said Gwen, in a smug voice. "She thinks too much of herself. I can't *think* why she's attached herself to me all these weeks."

Alicia couldn't resist this. "Like calls to like, dear Gwen," she said. "Deep calls to deep. You're as like as two peas, you and Maureen. It's been a sweet sight to see you together."

"You don't really mean that, Alicia?" said Gwen, after a surprised and hurt silence. "We're not *really* alike, Maureen and I. You've let your tongue run away with you as usual."

"Think about it, dear Gwendoline Mary," Alicia advised her. "Do you babble endlessly about your dull family and doings? So does Maureen. Do you think the world of yourself? So does Maureen. Do you think you'd be the one and only person fit to be Cinderella in the play? So does Maureen."

Gwen sprang to her feet and pointed her finger at Moira. "Oh! Just because you found me with my hair down in the dormy the other day, and a towel round my shoulders you went and told the others that I wanted to be Cinderella!"

"Well, I didn't realize it until I caught Maureen doing exactly the same thing," said Moira. "*Both* of you posing with your hair loose and things draped round you! Alicia's perfectly right. You're as like as two peas. You *ought* to be friends. You're almost twins!"

"But – I don't *like* Maureen," said Gwen, in a loud and angry tone.

"I'm not surprised," said Alicia's smooth voice, a whole wealth of meaning in it. "*You* should know what she's like, shouldn't you – seeing that you're almost twins!"

Gwen went stamping out of the room, fuming. Darrell drummed on the table with a pencil. "I'm not awfully pleased about all this," she said, in rather a small voice. "Too much spite and malice about!"

Gwen suddenly put her head in at the door again and addressed Moira.

"I'll get even with you for telling the girls about me and Maureen in front of the glass!" she said. "You'll see – I'll pay you back, head girl or no head girl!"

Moira frowned and Belinda automatically reached for her pencil. A very fine scowl! But Darrell took the pencil away with a beseeching look.

"Not this time," she said. "There's too much spite in this room this evening."

"All right – Saint Darrell!" said Belinda, and Darrell had to laugh.

Moira came over to her. "Let's change the subject," she said. "What about the house matches? Let's have a look at the kids you've put in."

Darrell got out the lists. Moira, as head girl, took an interest in the matches in which the fifth-formers played, and because she liked games, she was interested too in the lower-school players. It was about the only thing that she and Darrell saw eye to eye about.

Soon they were deep in discussion, weighing up the merits of one player against another.

"This match against Wellsbrough," said Darrell. "Next week's match, I mean, with the fourth team playing Wellsbrough's fourth team. I've put young Susan in – and I'd *like* to put my young sister, Felicity, in, what do you think, Moira?"

"Good gracious, *yes*," said Moira. "She's absolutely first class. Super! Runs like the wind and never misses a catch. She must have been practising like anything!"

"She has," said Darrell. "I just hesitated because – well, because she's my sister, and I was a bit afraid I might be showing favouritism, you know."

"Rot!" said Moira. "You'd be showing yourself a bad captain if you didn't stick the best kids into the team! And I insist on your putting Felicity in!"

Darrell laughed. She was pleased. "Oh, all right, seeing that you insist!" she said, and wrote Felicity's name down. "Gosh, she'll be pleased."

"How's June shaping?" called Alicia. "I've seen her practising quite a bit lately. Turning over a new leaf do you think?"

"Well – not really," said Darrell. "I mean – she practises a lot – but when I coach her she's as offhand as ever. Never a word of thanks, and always ready to argue. I can't put her into a match team yet. She simply doesn't understand the team spirit – you know, always plays for herself, and not for the side."

"Yes, you're right," said Moira. "I've noticed that, too. Can't have anyone in the team who isn't willing to pull their weight."

Darrell glanced curiously at Moira. *How* much nicer Moira was over this games question than over anything else! She was fair and just and interested. She forgot to be domineering and opinionated. What a pity she was head of the form – she might have been so much nicer if she had had to knuckle down to someone else.

"Could you take the lists down for me and put them up on the sports board?" she said to Moira. "I've got a whole heap of things to do still."

Moira took the list just as Catherine hurried to offer to take it. "*I'll* take it," said Catherine, who seemed to think it was only right she should be a doormat for everyone.

"No, thanks, Saint Catherine," said Moira, and Catherine went red with humiliation. She had done so much for Moira, been so nice to her, taken such a lot of donkey work off her shoulders – and all she got was that scornful, hateful name – Saint Catherine. She gave Moira an unexpectedly spiteful look.

Darrell saw it and shivered impatiently. "I don't like all this spitefulness going about," she thought to herself. "It always boils up into something beastly. Fancy the saintly Catherine giving her beloved Moira such a poisonous look!"

Moira went down with the lists. She pinned the list of names for the Fourth Team up first, heading it: "TEAM FOR WELLSBROUGH MATCH". Immediately a crowd of excited first-formers swarmed round her.

"Felicity! You're in, you're in!" yelled somebody, and Felicity's face glowed happily.

"So's Susan. But you're not, June," said another voice. "Fancy – and you've been practising so hard. Shame!"

"Oh well – what do you expect – Darrell would be *sure* to put her sister in," said June's voice. She was bitterly disappointed, but she spoke in her usual jaunty manner.

Moira heard. "June! Apologize at once; Darrell shows no favouritism at all. She was half inclined to leave Felicity out. *I* insisted she should be put in. Apologize immediately."

"Well," began June, defiantly, ready to argue, but Moira was insistent.

"I said, 'Apologize'. You heard me. Do as you're told."

"I apologize," said June, sulkily. "But I bet it was you who missed *me* out!"

"I told Darrell that I wouldn't have anyone in the match team who didn't play for the team and not for themselves," said Moira, curtly. "You don't pull your weight. You practise and practise – and then in a game all you want to do is to go your own way, and blow the others! Not *my* idea of a good sportsman. Think about it, June."

She walked off, not caring in the least what the first-formers thought of her outspokenness. June said nothing. She looked rather odd, Susan thought. She went up to her.

"It was mean to say all that in front of us," she began. "She should have . . . "

"What does it matter?" said June, suddenly jaunty again. "Do you suppose I care tuppence for Moira, or Darrell or Alicia – or *any* of those stuck-up fifth-formers?"

Grand Meeting

A grand meeting was called to discuss the panto-mime, the casting of the characters, and the times of rehearsal. Darrell had finished her writing, and Irene had completed the music. Everything was ready for rehearsal.

All the fifth-formers attended the meeting in the North Tower common room. It was very crowded. A fire burned in the big fire place, for it was now October and the nights were cold.

Moira was in the chair. Catherine – rather a quiet and sulky Catherine, not quite so free with her beaming smile – was at her left hand, ready to provide her with anything she wanted. The committee sat on chairs on each side of the table.

Moira banged on the table with a book, and shouted for silence. She got it. People always automatically obeyed Moira! She had that kind of voice, crisp and curt.

The meeting began. Darrell was called upon to explain the pantomime and the characters in it. She was also asked to read the first act.

Very flushed and excited she gave the listening fifth-formers a short summary of the pantomime. They listened with much approval. It sounded very good.

Then, stammering a little at first, Darrell read the first act of the pantomime, just as she had written it, dialogue, songs, stage directions and everything. There was a deep silence as she read on.

"That's the end of the act," she said at last, raising her eyes half-shyly, not absolutely certain if she had carried her listeners with her or not.

There was no doubt about that a second later. The girls stamped and clapped and cheered. Darrell was so pleased that she felt hot with joy, and had to wipe her forehead dry.

Moira banged for silence.

"Well, you've all heard what a jolly good play Darrell and Sally have got together," she said. "Darrell did most of it – but Sally was splendid too. You can tell it will bring the house down if we can produce it properly."

"Who's going to produce it?" called Betty.

"I am," said Moira, promptly. "Any objections?"

There were quite a lot of doubtful faces. Nobody really doubted Moira's ability to produce a pantomime – but they did doubt her talent for getting the best out of people. She rubbed them up the wrong way so much.

"I think it would be better to have *two* producers," said somebody.

"Right," said Moira, promptly. She didn't mind how many there were so long as she was one of them. She meant to be the *real* producer, anyway. "Who do you want?"

"Betty, Betty!" shrieked half the fifth-formers. It was obviously planned. Moira frowned a little. Betty! Alicia's laughing, careless, clever friend.

"Yes – let Betty," said Alicia, suddenly. She felt that she wouldn't be able to work happily with Moira alone for long. But two producers would be easier. She could consult with Betty all the time!

Betty grinned round and took her place on one of the committee chairs. "Thanks," she said. "I'll produce the goods all right!"

"Now to choose the characters," said Moira. "We have more or less worked them out. I'll read them."

Gwendoline and Maureen held their breath. *Was* there any hope of being Cinderella? Or even the Fairy Godmother? Or the Prince?

Moira read the list out.

"Cinderella – *Mary-Lou.*"

There was a gasp from Mary-Lou, Gwen and Maureen – of amazement from Mary-Lou and disappointment from the others.

"Oh – I *can't*!" said Mary-Lou.

"You *can*," said Darrell. "We want someone sort

of pathetic-looking – a bit scared – someone appealing and big-eyed – and it has to be someone who can act and someone who can sing."

"And you're exactly right for the part," said Sally. "That's right – make your eyes big and scared, Mary-Lou – you're poor little Cinderella to the life!"

Everyone laughed. Mary-Lou had to laugh, too. Her eyes began to shine. "I never thought you'd choose me," she said.

"Well, we have," said Darrell. "You can act very well and you've a nice singing voice, though it's not very loud."

"The Prince – *Mavis*," said Moira. Everyone knew that already. The Prince had a lot of singing to do and Mavis would do that wonderfully well. Her voice was beautiful again, and Irene had written some lovely tunes for her to sing to Darrell's words. Everyone clapped.

"The Baron – *Bill*," said Moira, and there was a delighted laugh.

"Oh yes! Bill stamping about in riding-breeches, calling for her horse!" cried Clarissa in delight.

"Fairy Godmother – *Louella*," said Moira. Everyone looked at Louella who came from South Tower, and had a tall, slim figure, golden curls and a good clear voice.

"Hurray!" shouted all the South Tower girls, glad to have someone from their tower in a good part.

"Buttons – the little boots – *Rachel*!" went on Moira. "Rachel can act jolly well and she's had the same part before, so she ought to do it well."

"Who are the Ugly Sisters?" called a voice.

Gwen's heart suddenly gave a lurch and sank down into her shoes. Ugly Sisters! Suppose *she* had been chosen to be one? She couldn't, couldn't bear it. She saw Alicia gazing at her maliciously and felt sure she

100

had been chosen.

She simply couldn't bear it. She got up, saying she didn't feel very well, and went towards the door. Alicia smiled. She could read Gwen's thoughts extremely well. Gwen was going because she was afraid her name would be read out next as one of the Ugly Sisters.

"Your heart worrying you again?" called one of the West Tower girls to Gwen, and everyone laughed. Gwen disappeared. She made up her mind not to go back till the meeting was over.

Maureen was also worried about the same thing. She thought about her rabbit-teeth. Moira might think she was *made* for an Ugly Sister. Why, oh why hadn't she been sensible and had her teeth straightened when she had a chance? She drew her upper lip over them to try and hide them.

"Ugly Sisters – *Pat* and *Rita*!" said Moira, and there was an instant roar of approval from the girls.

Pat and Rita looked round humorously. They were twins, and certainly not ugly – but they had upturned comical noses, eyes very wide-set and hair that flew out in a shock. They were comical, good at acting, and would make a splendid pair of Ugly Sisters.

"Thanks, Moira!" called out Rita. "That suits us down to the ground – right down to our big ugly feet!"

"Demon King – *Alicia*!" said Moira, and again there was a great roar of approval, led by a delighted Betty.

Moira beamed round, looking quite pleasant. "Alicia's going to do juggling and conjuring as well as leap about the stage like a demon," she said. "I can't think of anyone else who could be a demon so successfully."

More shrieks of approval. Miss James, not far off, wondered what in the world was happening.

101

It sounded as if about fifty thousand spectators at a football match were yelling themselves hoarse.

"Jolly good casting!" called somebody. "Go on!"

"Well, now we come to the servants and courtiers and so on," said Moira. "That means the rest of you. There's a part for everyone, even though it may be small."

"What about Darrell?" called a voice.

"Darrell's written the play and will help in the producing," said Moira. "Sally will help her too. They won't be in it because their hands will be full. We're going to ask Pop if he'll do the electricity part – he'll love it."

Pop was the handyman of the school, very much beloved, and quite invaluable on these occasions.

"It all sounds jolly good," said Winnie. "When are the rehearsals?"

"Every Tuesday evening, and on Friday evenings too for those who want an extra one," said Moira. "And the parts will be sent out to everyone tomorrow. For goodness' sake learn them as quickly as you can. It's hopeless to keep reading them when we rehearse – you can't act properly like that."

"You forgot to say that Irene's done the music and Belinda the decorations and Janet's doing the costumes," said Darrell.

"No, I hadn't," said Moira, quickly. "I was coming to that. Anyway, everyone knows it. By the way, we'll be glad of any help for Janet in making the costumes. Anyone good with their needle will be welcomed. Janet will give out the work if you'll be decent enough to ask her for it."

More clapping. Then a spate of excited talk. This was going to be the best pantomime ever! It would make the whole school sit up! It would bring the house down.

"There's never been a show before where the girls wrote the songs and words and music themselves," said Winnie. "My word – won't the Grayling open her eyes!"

A bell went somewhere and everyone got up. "We'll be at rehearsal! We'll learn our parts! Mavis, what about the singing? Are you going to train the chorus?"

Chattering and calling they all went to their own towers. Darrell sighed happily and put her arm through Sally's.

"This is about the most exciting thing I've ever done in my life, Sally," she said. "You know – I shouldn't be surprised if I don't turn out to be a writer, one of these days!"

Felicity's First Match

Felicity came to see Darrell the next day about the match with Wellsbrough School. She looked with bright eyes at her fifth-form sister.

"I *say*! Fancy me playing in the Fourth School Team! I thought perhaps I might by the end of term, with luck – but next *week*! Thanks awfully for putting me in, Darrell."

"Well, actually – it was Moira who insisted on putting you in," said Darrell. "I wanted to – and yet I just wondered if I was thinking favourably of you because you were my sister, you know. Then Moira said you must certainly go in, and in you went."

"June's awfully disappointed she's not in," said

Felicity. "She's been practising like anything, Darrell. She pretends she doesn't care, but she does really. I wish she wouldn't say such awful things about you fifth-formers all the time – she really seems to have got her knife into you. It's horrid."

"She'll get over it," said Darrell. "We don't lose any sleep over young June, I can tell you!"

"Will you be able to come and watch the Wells-brough match?" asked Felicity, eagerly. "Oh do. I shall play so much better if you're there, yelling and cheering."

"Of course I'll come," said Darrell. "And I'll yell like anything – so just be sure you give me something to yell for!"

The first-formers prayed for a fine day for their match. It was to be at home, not away, and as it was the first time they had played Wellsbrough Fourth Team, they were really excited about it.

The senior school smiled to see the "babies" so excited. They remembered how they, too, had felt when they had the delight of playing in an important match for the very first time.

"Nice to see them so keen," said Moira to Darrell. "I think I'll get my lacrosse stick and go and give them a bit of coaching before dinner. I've got half an hour."

"I'll fetch your stick," said Catherine at once, in her usual doormat voice.

"No thanks, Saint Catherine," answered Moira, "I'm still able to walk to the locker and reach my own stick."

The day of the match dawned bright and clear, a magnificent October day. The trees round the playing fields shone red and brown and yellow in their autumn colours. The breeze from the sea was salty and crisp. All the girls rejoiced as they got up that morning and looked out of the window. Malory Towers was so lovely on a day like this.

The happiest girls, of course, were the small first-formers, excited twelve-year-olds who talked to one another at the tops of their voices without stopping. How they ever heard what anyone else said was a mystery.

Miss Potts, the first-form mistress, was lenient that morning. So was Mam'zelle who was always excited herself when any of her classes were.

"Well, so today is your match?" she said to the first form. "You will play well, *n'est-ce pas?* You will win all the goals. I shall come to watch. And for the girl that wins a goal . . . "

"*Shoots* a goal, Mam'zelle," said Susan.

"Shoots! Ah yes – but you have no gun to shoot a goal," said Mam'zelle, who never could learn the language of sports. "Well, well – for the girl who *shoots* a goal I will say 'no French prep tomorrow'!"

"But, Mam'zelle – that's not fair!" cried a dozen voices. "We're not *all* in the match – only Felicity and Susan and Vera."

"Ah, I forgot," said Mam'zelle. "That is so. Then what shall I say?"

"Say you'll let us *all* off French prep for the rest of the week if we win!" called Felicity.

"No, no," said Mam'zelle, shocked. "For one day only I said. Now, it is understood – if you win your match no French prep for you tomorrow!"

"You're a peach, Mam'zelle," called a delighted first-former.

"*Comment!*" said Mam'zelle, astonished. "You call me a *peach*. Never have I . . . "

"It's all right, Mam'zelle – it's a compliment," said Felicity. "Peaches are wizard."

Mam'zelle gave it up. "Now – we will have our

verbs," she said. "Page thirty-five, *s'il vous plaît*, and no more talking."

The Wellsbrough girls arrived at twenty past two in a big coach. They were rather older than the Malory Towers team, and seemed much bigger. The Malory Towers girls felt a little nervous. The two captains shook hands and the teams nodded and smiled at one another.

The games mistress blew her whistle and the teams came round her. The captains tossed for ends.

The teams took their positions in the field. Felicity gripped her lacrosse stick as if it might leap from her hand if she didn't. She put on a grim expression that made everyone who saw it smile.

Her knees shook just a little! How she hoped nobody could see them. It was silly to be nervous in a match – just the time *not* to be!

"Good luck," whispered Susan, who was not far off. "Shoot a goal!"

Felicity nodded, still looking grim.

Darrell and Moira and Sally were together, watching. Most of the other fifth-formers were there, too, because many of them helped the younger ones and were interested in their play. A good sprinkling of the other forms were also there. Wellsbrough was a splendid school for sport and usually sent out first class match teams.

"Your small sister looks pretty fierce," said Sally to Darrell. "Look at her! She seems to do and dare all right!"

The match began. The ball shot out down the field, and the girls began to race after it, picking it up in their nets, throwing it, catching it, knocking it out again, picking it up, tackling one another and making the onlookers yell with excitement.

The Wellsbrough team shot the first goal. It went

clean into the net, quite impossible to stop. The twelve-year-old goalkeeper was very downcast. One to Wellsbrough!

Felicity gritted her teeth. Wellsbrough had the lead now. She shot a look at Darrell. Yes, there she was, never taking her eyes off the ball. Felicity longed to do something really spectacular and make Darrell dance and cheer with pride. But the Wellsbrough team was tough, and nobody could do anything very startling. Always there was a Wellsbrough girl ready to knock the ball out of a Malory Towers lacrosse net as soon as it was there!

And always there was a Wellsbrough girl who seemed to be able to run faster than any of the home team. It was maddening. Felicity and Susan became very out of breath and panted and puffed as they tore down the field, their hearts beating like pistons!

And then Susan shot a goal! It was most unexpected. She was tearing down the field, far from the goal, with two Wellsbrough girls after her, and Felicity running up to catch the ball if Susan passed it.

Susan took a quick glance round to see if Felicity was ready to catch it. A Wellsbrough girl ran up beside Felicity, a tall girl who would probably take the ball instead of Felicity, if it was passed. Blow!

On the spur of the moment Susan flung the ball at the distant goal. It was a powerful throw, and the ball flew straight. The goalkeeper rushed out to catch it – but she missed, and the ball bounced right into the very middle of the net!

Cheers rang out from the spectators. Darrell yelled too. Then she turned to Moira.

"A very lucky goal. Those far throws don't usually come off – but that one did. One all!"

It was almost half-time. One minute to go. The

ball came to Felicity and she caught it deftly in her net, jumping high in the air for it.

"Good!" yelled everyone, pleased to see such a fine catch. Felicity sped off with it and passed to Rita. She didn't see a big Wellsbrough girl running up to her and collided heavily. Over she went on the ground and felt an agonizing pain in her right ankle. It was so sharp that she couldn't get up. Things went black around her. Poor Felicity was horrified. No, no, she mustn't faint! Not on the playing-field in the middle of the match! She couldn't!

The whistle went for half-time. Felicity heaved a long shaky sigh of relief. Five minutes' rest. Would her ankle be all right?

She wasn't going to faint after all! She sat there on the grass, pretending to fiddle with her lacrosse boot till she felt a little better. Susan came running up.

"I say – you went over with a terrific wallop. Did you hurt yourself?"

"Twisted my ankle a little," said Felicity. She looked very white and Susan was alarmed. The games mistress came up.

"Twisted your ankle? Let's have a look."

She undid the boot quickly and looked at Felicity's foot, pressing it and turning it.

"It's an ordinary twist," she said. "Horribly painful when it happens, I know. You'd better come off and let your reserve play."

Felicity was almost in tears. Darrell came running up. "Has she twisted her ankle? Oh, she often does that. Her right ankle's a bit weak. Daddy always tells her to bandage it fairly tightly – round the foot just here – and walk on it immediately, not lie up."

"Well, I'm agreeable to that if Felicity can stand on it all right, and run," said the mistress. "It's up to her."

Susan brought Felicity a lemon quarter to suck. She began to feel much better and colour came back into her cheeks. She stood up, testing her ankle gingerly. Then she smiled.

"It's all right. It will be black and blue tomorrow, but there's nothing really wrong. In a few minutes' time it will be better."

The games mistress bound the foot up tightly, and Felicity put on her boot again. The foot had swollen a little but not much. Chewing her lemon, Felicity hobbled about for a minute or two, feeling the foot getting better and better as she went.

"Nothing much wrong," reported the games mistress. "A nasty twist – but Felicity's a determined little character, and where another girl would moan and make a fuss and go off limping, she's going to go on playing. It won't do the foot any harm – probably do it good."

The whistle went again, after a little longer half-time to give Felicity a chance to recover. The girls took their places, all at the opposite ends this time.

Susan was a marvel that second half. She saved Felicity all she could, and leapt about and ran like a mad March hare! Everyone cheered her.

Felicity's foot ceased to hurt her. She forgot about it. She began to run again, and made another wonderful catch that set all the spectators cheering. She tackled a Wellsbrough girl and got the ball away. She ran for goal.

"Shoot!" yelled everyone. "SHOOT!"

But, before she could shoot, the ball was knocked out of her net and a Wellsbrough girl was speeding back down the field with it. She passed the ball on, and it was caught and passed again, and shot straight at the Malory Towers goal.

"Save it, save it!" yelled everyone in agony. The

goalkeeper stood there like a rock. She made a wild slash with her lacrosse stick and miraculously caught the hard rubber ball, flinging it out to a Malory Towers girl at once.

"No goal, no goal!" sang the girls in delight. "Well saved, Hilda, well saved!"

"Looks as if it's going to be a draw," said Moira, glancing at her watch. "Only two minutes more. Felicity's limping just a bit again. Plucky kid to run on as she did."

"She's got the ball!" cried Darrell, clutching Moira in excitement. "Another marvellous catch! My word, practice does pay! She catches better than anyone. Look, she's kept it!"

Felicity was running down the field with the ball. She was tackled by a Wellsbrough girl, dodged, turned herself right round and passed to Susan. Susan caught it and immediately passed it back to Felicity, seeing two of the enemy coming straight at her. Felicity nearly didn't catch it, because it was such a high throw, but by leaping like a goat she got it into the tip of her net, and it ran down safely.

Then off she went, tearing down the field, her face set grimly.

"SHOOT!" yelled the girls. "SHOOOOOOOOT!"

And she shot, just as the stick of an enemy came crashing down to get the ball from her. The ball shot out high in the air, and the goalkeeper rushed out to get it.

She missed it – and the ball bounced and ran slowly and deliberately into a corner of the goal, where it lay still as if quite tired out with the game.

"GOAL!" yelled everyone, and went completely mad. Moira, Sally and Darrell swung each other round in a most undignified way for fifth-formers, Bill and Clarissa did a kind of barn dance together, and as for the lower school, they began a most deafening chant that made Mam'zelle put her hands to her ears at once.

"Well – done – Felici-TEEEEEE! Well – done – Felici-TEEEEEE!"

The whistle went for time. The teams trooped off, red in the face, panting, laughing and happy. Felicity was limping a little, but so happy and proud that she wouldn't have noticed if she had limped with *both* feet!

Darrell thumped her on the back. "You got the winning goal, my girl! You did the trick! Gosh, I'm proud of you!"

Moira thumped her, too. "I'm glad we put you into the team, Felicity! You'll be there for the rest of the term. You've got team spirit all right. You play for your side all the time."

June was just nearby. She heard what Moira said, and felt sure she was saying it so that she might hear. She turned away, sick at heart. *She* might have been playing in the match – she might even have shot that winning goal. But Felicity had instead. June couldn't go and thump Felicity on the back or congratulate her. She was jealous.

Felicity was too happy to notice little things like that. She went off with her team and the Wellsbrough girls to a "smashing" tea. Anyone seeing the piles of sandwiches, buttered and jammy buns, and slices of fruit cake piled high on big dishes would think that surely it would need twenty teams to eat all that!

But the two teams managed it all between them quite easily. What fun it all was! What a noise of shouting and laughter and wholehearted merriment.

"School's smashing," thought Felicity, munching her fourth jammy bun. "Super! Wizard!"

Rehearsals began. A Tuesday and a Friday came, and another Tuesday – three rehearsals already!

"I think it's going well, don't you?" said Darrell to Sally. "Little Mary-Lou knows her part already – she must have slaved at learning it, because Cinderella has almost more to say than anyone."

"Yes – and she's going to look the part *exactly*," said Sally. "Who would ever have thought that timid little Mary-Lou, who was scared even of her own shadow when she was in the lower school, would be able to take the principal part in a pantomime now!"

"Shows what Malory Towers does to you!" said Darrell. "Still, I suppose any good boarding school does the same things – makes you stand on your own feet, rubs off your corners, teaches you common-sense, makes you accept responsibility."

"It depends on the person!" said Sally, with a laugh. "It doesn't seem to have taught dear Gwendoline Mary much."

"Well, I suppose there must be exceptions," said Darrell. "She's about the only one that's come up the school with us who doesn't seem to have learnt anything sensible at all."

"It was a shock when we told her she and Maureen might be twins!" said Sally. "She really saw herself then as others see her. Anyway, I think she *is* better than she was – especially since she's had to go in for games and gym properly."

"She doesn't like being a servant in the play,"

said Darrell, with one of her wide grins. "Nor does Maureen. They've neither of them got a word to say in the play, and not much to do either – but as they both act so badly, it's just as well!"

"It's an awful blow to their pride," said Sally. "I say – Bill's going to be good, isn't she? She's the surly baron to the life as she strides about the stage in her riding boots, and slaps her whip against her side!"

Yes – the play was really going quite well. The fifth-formers were almost sorry that it was half term weekend because it meant missing a rehearsal that Friday. Still, it would be lovely to see their parents again. Darrell had a lot to tell hers – and so had Felicity.

Felicity's ankle had certainly been black and blue the next day, and she showed it off proudly to the first-formers. What a marvel to shoot a goal when you had an ankle like that! Felicity was quite the heroine of the lower school.

Half term came and went, all too quickly. Darrell's father and mother came, and had to listen to two excited girls both talking at once about pantomimes and matches.

"We're rehearsing well, and my words sound fine, and you should see Mary-Lou as Cinderella," cried Darrell at the top of her voice.

"And when I shot the winning goal I simply couldn't believe it, but there was such a terrific noise of cheering and shouting that I had to," shouted Felicity, at the same time as Darrell. Her mother smiled. What a pair!

Four of Bill's brothers came to see her, and her mother as well, all on horseback! It was the boys' half term, too, and Bill rode off happily, taking Clarissa with her. "What a lovely way to spend half term," thought Clarissa, "riding all day long, and having a picnic lunch and tea!"

Gwendoline watched her go jealously. If she had been sensible last term she could have been Clarissa's friend. But she hadn't been sensible – and now she was stuck with that awful Maureen!

The dreadful thing was that Maureen's parents couldn't come at the last moment, so Maureen had no one to go out with. She went to tell Gwen.

"Oh, Gwen – are you taking anyone out with you? My parents can't come. I'm so bitterly disappointed."

Gwen stared at her crossly. This *would* happen, of course. Now she would have to have Maureen tagging about with her all day long.

She introduced Maureen to her mother and Miss Winter, her old governess, with a very bad grace.

"Mother – this is Maureen. Her parents haven't come today, so I said she could come with us."

"Of course, of course!" said Mrs Lacy at once. As usual she was dressed in far too fussy things, with veils and scarves and bits and pieces flying everywhere. "Poor child – what a shame!"

Maureen warmed to Mrs Lacy. Here was someone she could talk to easily. She gave her silly little laugh.

"Oh, Mrs Lacy, it's *so* kind of you to let me come with you. It's my first term here, you know – and really I don't know *what* I'd have done without dear Gwendoline. She's really been a friend in need."

"I'm sure she has," said Mrs Lacy. "Gwendoline is always so kind. No wonder she is so popular."

"And do you know, the girls say Gwen and I *ought* to be friends, because we're so alike," chattered Maureen, tucking the rug round herself in the car. "We've both got golden hair and blue eyes, and they say we've got the same ways, too. Aren't I lucky to have found a twin!"

This was the kind of conversation that both Miss Winter and Mrs Lacy understood and liked. Miss

Winter made quite a fuss of Maureen, and Gwen didn't like that at all.

Gwen hoped that Maureen would say nice things about her as she was taking her out for the day. But Maureen didn't. Maureen talked about herself the whole time. She described her home, her family, her dogs, her garden, all the holidays she had ever had, and all the illnesses. Gwen couldn't get a word in, and after a time she fell silent and sulked.

"What a bore Maureen is! How silly! How selfish and conceited!" thought Gwen, sulkily. "What a silly affected laugh."

Her mother made a most terrifying remark at lunch time. She beamed round at both girls. "You know, except that Maureen's teeth stick out a little, you two are really *very* alike! You've got Gwen's lovely way of chattering all about your doings, Maureen – and even your laugh is the same – isn't it, Miss Winter?"

"Yes, they really might be sisters," agreed Miss Winter, smiling kindly at the delighted Maureen. "Their ways are exactly the same, and even their voices."

Gwen felt quite sick. She could hardly eat any lunch. If her mother and Miss Winter, who really adored her, honestly thought that that awful, boring, conceited Maureen was exactly like her, then she, Gwen, must be a really appalling person too. No wonder she wasn't popular. No wonder the girls laughed at her.

That day was a really terrible one for Gwen. To sit by somebody who was supposed to be like her, to hear her own silly laugh uttered by Maureen, to listen to her everlasting, dull tales about herself, and see her own shallow, insincere smile spread over Maureen's face was a horrible experience.

"I shall never forget this," thought poor Gwen.

"Never. I'll be jolly careful how I behave in future. And I'll alter my laugh straight away. Do I *really* laugh like that? Yes – I do. Oh, I do feel so ashamed."

"Gwen's very quiet," said Miss Winter, at last. "Anything wrong, Gwen?"

"Oh, poor Gwen – she's so disappointed because she's not chosen for Cinderella," said Maureen, swiftly.

"Well, so were you!" retorted Gwen. "*You* thought you were going to be. Moira said so!"

"Girls, girls! Don't talk like that to one another," said Mrs Lacy, shocked. "Why – I quite thought Gwen was to be Cinderella!"

"Yes – you said in your letter that most of the girls wanted you to be," said Miss Winter. "Why didn't they choose you, Gwen? You would have made a fine Cinderella! It's a shame."

"For the same reason they didn't choose Maureen, I suppose," said Gwen, sulkily. "They didn't think we were good enough."

"Well, of course, I couldn't *possibly* expect to be chosen – it's only my first term," said Maureen, quickly.

"You *did* expect to be!" said Gwen.

"Oh no, Gwen dear," said Maureen, and laughed her silly laugh. It grated on Gwen's exasperated nerves.

"I shall go mad if you laugh that laugh again," she said, savagely.

There was a surprised silence. Maureen broke it by laughing again and Gwen clenched her fists.

"Poor Gwen!" said Maureen. "Honestly, Mrs Lacy it *was* a shame they didn't choose her – it really did upset her. And when we go to rehearsals it's maddening for Gwen to see Mary-Lou as Cinderella, whilst she's only a servant, and says nothing at all – not a single word in the whole of the play!"

"Darling!" said Mrs Lacy, comfortingly, to the glowering Gwen. "I'm *so* sorry! I don't like to see Mother's girl sad."

"*Stop* it, Mother," said Gwen. "Let's change the subject."

Mrs Lacy was very hurt. She turned away from this unusually surly Gwen, and began to talk to Maureen, being extra nice to her so as to show Gwen that she was very displeased with *her*. Miss Winter did the same, and Maureen blossomed out even more under this sunshine of flattery and rapt attention. Poor Gwen had to listen to more and more tales of Maureen's life, and to hear her silly laugh more and more often!

The day came to an end at last. Maureen thanked Mrs Lacy and Miss Winter prettily, tucked her arm into Gwen's, and went off, waving.

"I'll look after Gwen for you!" she called back.

"Well, *what* a charming child – and *what* a nice friend she'd make for Gwen," said Mrs Lacy, driving off. "It's a pity Gwen's so upset about that Cinderella business. Maureen must have been just as disappointed."

"Yes. I'm afraid dear Gwen's not taking that very bravely," said Miss Winter. "Never mind, she has that nice child Maureen to set her a good example."

"I think we ought to ask Maureen to stay for a week or two in the Christmas holidays," said Mrs Lacy. "It would be so nice for Gwen."

Poor Gwen! If she had heard all this she would have been furious. She was to get a great shock when her mother's letter came, telling her she had invited Maureen to stay for a week in the holidays.

She pulled her arm away from Maureen's as soon as the car drove out of sight. She turned on her.

"Well – I hope you've enjoyed spoiling my whole day, you beast! Telling your awful tales, and laughing your awful laugh, and sucking up like anything. Ugh!"

"But, Gwen – they said I was so like you," said Maureen, looking puzzled. "They liked me. How can I be so awful if I'm exactly like you?"

Gwen didn't tell her. It was a thing she really couldn't bear to think about.

The Dictator

The days began to fly after half term. Darrell and Sally got fits of panic quite regularly whenever they thought of the pantomime being performed to the parents at the end of term.

"We'll NEVER be ready!" groaned Darrell.

"No. We never imagined there'd be so much to do," said Sally, seriously.

"If only everyone knew their parts like Mary-Lou and Mavis," said Darrell. "Louella drives me mad. She forgets the words of her songs every single time. I wish we hadn't chosen her to be the fairy godmother now."

"Oh, she'll be all right on the night," said Sally. "She was like that in the play she was in last year – never knew a word till the last night, and then was quite perfect."

"Well, I only hope you're right," groaned Darrell, amusing the steady Sally very much. Darrell went down into the dumps easily over her precious pantomime. Sally was very good for her. She refused to think anyone was hopeless, and was always ready with something comforting to say.

119

"Alicia's marvellous, isn't she?" she said, after a pause, looking up from the work she was doing.

"Yes. She's a born demon," said Darrell, with a giggle. "I get quite scared of her sometimes, the way she leaps about the stage and yells. And her conjuring is miraculous."

"So is her juggling," said Sally. "And she's practised that demon-sounding voice till it really sounds quite uncanny."

Daphne joined in with a laugh. "Yes – and when she suddenly produces it in French class, the amazement on Mam'zelle's face is too good to be true."

"Alicia's a scream," said Darrell. "She'll be the best in the show, I think."

There was a little silence. "There's only one thing that *really* worries me," said Darrell, in a low voice. "And that's Moira. She's not hitting it off with Betty at all – or Alicia either. She's bossing them too much."

"Yes. She can't seem to help it," said Sally. "But it's idiotic to be bossy with people like Betty and Alicia. After all, Betty's co-producer, and Alicia's a terrific help to them."

Darrell was right to worry about Moira. Moira was intensely keen on getting the whole pantomime perfect, and made everyone work like slaves under her command. The girls resented it. Louella purposely forgot her words in order to annoy Moira. Bill purposely came in at the wrong side each time to make her shout. And Moira couldn't see that she was handling things in the wrong way.

She was a wonderful organizer, certainly. She had gone into every detail, worked out every scene with Darrell, proved herself most ingenious, and given very wise advice.

But she did it all in the wrong way. She was aggressive and opinionated, she contradicted people flatly, and she found fault too much and praised too little.

"You're a dictator, Moira," Bill informed her at one rehearsal. "I don't take kindly to dictators. Nor does anyone else here."

"If you think you can produce a first class pantomime without giving a few orders and finding a few faults, you're wrong," said Moira, furiously.

"I don't," said Bill, mildly. "I never said I did. But you can do all that without being a dictator. You sit up there like a war-lord and chivy us all along unmercifully. I quite expect to be sent to prison sometimes."

"Let's get on," said Darrell, afraid that Moira was going to blow up. Arguing always wasted so much time. "We'll take that bit again. Mavis, begin your song."

Mavis sang, and a silence fell. What a lovely voice she had, low and pure and sweet. That would make the audience gasp! It wasn't often that a schoolgirl had a voice like that.

"We shall miss her when she leaves, and goes to study music and singing at the College of Music," thought Darrell. Mavis's song came to an end, and she stepped back to let Buttons come on and do her bit.

Yes, rehearsals were hard work, but they were fun, too. Sally and Darrell began to feel more confidence as time went on. Darrell surprised herself at times, when she suddenly saw something wrong with the lines of the play, and hurried to alter them.

"I know just what's wrong and what's right now," she thought, as she scribbled new lines. "I adore doing this pantomime – feeling it's mine because I wrote it all. I want to do a play next. *Could* I write one – perhaps just a short one for next term? Shall I ever, ever be a well-known playwright?"

Gwen was a sulky actor. She hated being stuck at the back in the chorus, dressed as a servant, with nothing to say or do by herself. Maureen was much more cheerful about it. She drove Gwen nearly mad by some of the things she said.

"Of course, *I* don't mind having such a small, insignificant part," she said. "But it's different for you, Gwen. You've been here for years, and I've not been even one term. You *ought* to have had a good part. I couldn't expect one."

Gwen growled.

"I shall write and tell your mother you are *awfully* good as a servant," went on Maureen. "I do think it's so kind of her to ask me to stay. Won't it be fun to be together so much, Gwen, in the hols?"

Gwen didn't answer. She was beginning to be a little afraid of Maureen. Maureen was silly and affected – but she had a cunning and sly side to her nature, too. So had Gwen, of course. She recognized it easily in Maureen because it was in herself too. That was the dreadful part of this forced friendship with Maureen. It was like being friends with yourself, and knowing all the false, silly, sly things that went on in your own mind.

Gwen did try to alter herself a bit, so that she wouldn't be like Maureen. She stopped her silly laugh and her wide, false smile. She stopped talking about herself too.

To her enormous annoyance nobody seemed to notice it. As a matter of fact, they took so little notice of her at all that if she had suddenly grown a moustache and worn riding boots they wouldn't have bothered. Who wanted to pay any attention to Gwen? She had never done anything to make herself liked or trusted so the best thing to do was to ignore her.

And ignore her they did, though poor Gwen was

doing her best to be sensible and likeable now. She had left it a bit too late!

Two more weeks went by, and then suddenly a row flared up at rehearsal. It began over a very silly little thing indeed, as big rows often do.

Alicia took it into her head to evolve a kind of demon-chant whenever she appeared or disappeared on the stage. She only thought of it a few minutes before rehearsal, and hadn't time to tell Darrell or Sally, so she thought she would just introduce the weird little chant without warning.

And she did. She appeared with her sudden, surprising leaps, chanting eerily. "Oo-woo-la, woo-la, riminy-ree, oo-woo-la . . . "

Moira rapped loudly. The rehearsal stopped.

"Alicia! What on earth's that? It's not in the script, as you very well know."

"Of course I know," said Alicia, annoyed as always by Moira's unnecessarily sharp tone. "I hadn't time to ask Darrell to put it in. I only thought of it just now."

"Well, we can't insert new things now," said Moira, coldly. "And in any case it's not for you to suggest extraordinary chants like that. If we'd wanted one we'd have got Darrell to write one in."

"Look here, Moira," said Alicia, losing her temper rapidly. "I'm not a first-former. I'm . . . "

Darrell interrupted hastily. "Moira, I think that's really a good idea of Alicia's. What do you think, Betty? I never thought of a chant like that for the demon – but it does sound very demon-like, and . . . "

"Yes," said Betty, anxious to go against Moira, and back up her friend Alicia. "Yes. It's a jolly fine idea. We'll have it."

Moira went up in smoke at once, in a way that a demon king himself might have envied!

123

She stood up, glowering. "You only say that, Betty, because you're Alicia's friend, and . . ."

"Shucks," said Betty, rudely.

Moira went on without stopping. "And Darrell only says it because she always backs up Alicia, too. Well, I'm chief producer, and I'm going to have my way over this. There'll be no demon-chant. Get on with the rehearsal."

Alicia was white. "I'm not performing any more tonight," she said, in a cold and angry voice. "You're quite stealing the performance yourself, aren't you, Moira? Wonderful demon queen you'd make, with that look on your face!"

It was so exactly what Moira did look like that there were quite a lot of guffaws. Alicia walked off the stage. Darrell was petrified. Sally took charge.

"Who's on next? Come on, Bill."

Bill came on the wrong side as usual, determined to flout Moira, too. She stalked in, her hands in her breeches pockets. She always wore riding things when she rehearsed. She said it made her feel more baronial!

"BILL! You know perfectly well you don't come in that side," shouted Moira, who also knew perfectly well that it was just Bill's way of showing that she sided with Alicia. Bill stood there like a dummy.

"Go back and come in the right side," ordered Moira, harshly.

"No. I'm going riding," said Bill. Quite simply and mildly, just like that! She walked off, humming, and Moira heard her calling to Clarissa.

"Clarissa! Come on! I'm not feeling fit for acting tonight. I want to do something energetic!"

"This is silly," said Betty. "Everyone walking off. Let *me* take charge, Moira. You're rubbing them up the wrong way tonight."

Moira shoved her roughly aside. She had a wicked

124

temper when she was really roused, the same kind of temper as her sister Bridget, who liked to smash things up if she really felt mad!

"I'm going on," she said, between her teeth. "Once we let things get out of hand, we're done. We'll take the servants' chorus."

The chorus came on, giggling and ready to play up Moira if they could. They all resented her hard ways, even though they admitted that she could get things done and done well.

Moira picked on Gwen and Maureen at once.

"You two! You're not singing! Oh no, you're not! So don't say you were. You're pretty awful every time, and you'd better pull your socks up now, or you won't even be in the chorus. I'll get some third-formers instead."

"I say! Do shut up, Moira," said Betty, in a low tone. "You know you'll never do much with those two, and certainly not if you go for them like that."

Moira took not the slightest notice. "Did you hear what I said, Gwen and Maureen?" she called. "Come out in front and sing by yourselves, so that I shall see if you *do* know the words."

Gwen hesitated. She longed to cheek Moira, or walk off as Bill had done. But she was afraid of Moira's sharp tongue.

"Very well then – stop where you are and sing there," said Moira, suddenly realizing that she couldn't very well go and drag Gwen and Maureen to the front by main force. "Music, please, Irene!"

Irene, looking very glum and disgusted, played the servants' chorus. Gwen's reedy voice piped up and Maureen mumbled the words, too.

"Stop," said Moira, and the music stopped. "You don't know the words and you don't know the tune –

and it is about the seventh rehearsal. You're the worst in the whole play, both of you."

Gwen and Maureen were furious at being humiliated like this in front of everyone. But still they dared not answer Moira back. They were both little cowards when it came to anything like that. They stood mute, and Gwen felt the usual easy tears welling up in her eyes.

Needless to say the rehearsal was not a success. Everyone sighed with relief when the supper bell went. Moira went off scowling. Many of the girls sent scowls after her in imitation.

"Beast," said Daphne. "She gets worse!"

"She's worried because she has so many rehearsals to take, and so much to do," said Darrell, trying to stop the general grumbling. It made things so difficult if the girls didn't come willingly and cheerfully to rehearsal. It was *her* pantomime, *her* masterpiece – she couldn't let their resentful feelings for Moira spoil it all.

"*Saint* Darrell!" called Betty, in delight. Darrell grinned.

"I'm no saint!" she said. "I'm as hot and bothered as everyone else. But what's the good of messing up the show just because we've got a producer who can't keep her temper?"

"Let's chuck her out," suggested somebody. "We've got Betty – and there's you and Sally and Alicia at hand to help. We don't need Moira now the donkey work is done."

"We can't possibly chuck her out," said Darrell, decidedly. "It would be mean after she's got it more or less into shape. I do honestly think she's irritable because she's so interested in getting it perfect, and every little thing upsets her. Give her another chance!"

126

"All right," agreed everyone. "But only ONE more chance, Darrell!"

The Anonymous Letters

Darrell spoke to Moira rather nervously about the failure of the last rehearsal.

"We all know you're a bit overworked because you've done so much for the show already," she began.

"Oh, do be quiet. You sound like Saint Catherine," said Moira, with a glance at the nearby Catherine.

"She's already tried to make a hundred silly excuses for me. I hate people who suck up. I wasn't angry because I was tired or overworked. I was angry because people like Alicia and Bill and Gwen and Maureen were defiant and rude and silly and lazy and didn't back me up. Now you know."

"Well, look, Moira – for goodness' sake be more understanding and patient next time," said Darrell, holding tight on to her own temper. She felt it suddenly rising up. Oh dear! It would never do for the two of them to get furious!

"Will you let me get on with my French or not?" asked Moira, in a dangerous voice. Darrell gave it up. The next rehearsal was a little better but not much. Darrell had insisted on writing in Alicia's chant, and Moira had frowned but said very little. After all, the script *was* Darrell's business. Moira didn't find any fault with either Alicia or Bill this time. She didn't need to. Both were admirable and knew their parts well. Bill, at Darrell's request, came on the stage from the right side, and all was well.

But other things went wrong. Other people came in for criticism and blame, the courtiers were ordered to sing their song four times, the servants didn't bow properly, or curtsy at the right moment, Buttons was talking when she shouldn't be!

Moira didn't lose her temper, but she was unpleasant and hard. She fought to keep herself in hand. She was head girl of the fifth. She was chief producer of the show. She had done all the donkey work and licked things into shape. She meant to have her own way, and to have things as she liked – and she wasn't going to say please and thank you and smile and clap, as that idiot of a Betty did!

There was a lot more grumbling afterwards. Darrell and Sally began to feel panicky. Suppose the pantomime went to pieces instead of getting perfect?

And then another horrid thing began. It was the coming of the anonymous letters – spiteful, hateful letters with no name at the end!

Only one girl in the form got them – and that was Moira. She got the first one on a rehearsal day. She slit open the envelope and read it in the common room. She exclaimed aloud in disgust.

"What's up?" said Darrell. Moira threw the letter across to her. "Read that," she said.

Darrell read it and was horrified. This was the letter:

If only you knew what people really think of the head girl of the fifth! Bad-tempered, unjust, bossy – if you left at the end of term it wouldn't be too soon for ME

"What a disgusting thing," said Darrell, in dismay. "Who could possibly have written it? It's all in printed capitals, to hide the writer's own handwriting. Take no notice of it, Moira. The only place for anonymous letters is the fire."

Moira tossed the note into the fire, and went on with her work. Nobody could tell if she was upset or not – but everyone wondered who had written such a horrible letter.

The next one arrived the following day. There it was, on top of Moira's pile of books, addressed in the same printed writing.

She opened it, unthinking.

So you got my first letter. I hope you enjoyed it. Wouldn't you love to know what the girls say about you? It would make your ears burn! You've certainly got the distinction of being the most unpopular girl in the school – but who wants that distinction? Certainly not

ME.

"Here's another of them," said Moira, in a casual tone, and gave it to Darrell and Sally. They read it, dismayed by the spite that lay behind the few lines.

"But, Moira – *who* can it be?" said Darrell. "Oh dear – it's horrible. Anonymous letters are always written by the lowest of the low, I feel – and it's awful to think there's someone like that at Malory Towers."

"*I* don't care," said Moira. But she did care. She remembered the spiteful words and worried over them in bed. She worried over the rehearsals, too. She badly wanted them to go as well as they had done at first – but poor Moira always found it very difficult to give up her own opinions and ways. She couldn't alter herself – she expected everyone else to adapt themselves to *her*. And they wouldn't, of course.

"Don't open any more notes," said Sally to Moira, seeing her look rather white the next day. "You know which they are – chuck them in the fire. You can tell

129

by the printing on the envelope what they are."

But the next one wasn't in an envelope. It was stuffed in Moira's lacrosse locker down in the changing room. It was actually inside her right boot! She took it out, and saw immediately what was written, for the note this time had no envelope.

What's a dictator? Ask Moira. Don't ask – ME.

Just that and no more. Moira crumpled up the note fiercely. This horrible letter-writer! She knew just what to say to hurt Moira most.

She told Darrell. She didn't really want to tell anyone, but somehow she felt she must put a brave front on the matter, and by telling about the letters and making them public she felt that would show the writer she didn't care.

She laughed as she showed Darrell the note. "Quite short this time," she said. "But not exactly sweet!"

"Oh! It's *hateful*!" said Darrell. "We *must* find out who it is. We *must* stop it. I've never, never known such a thing happen all the time I've been at Malory Towers. Poisonous, malicious letters! Moira, why aren't you more upset? I should be absolutely miserable if I got these! Even if I knew they weren't true," she added, hurriedly.

"You needn't add that," said Moira, with a faint smile. "They *are* true, actually. More than one of you have called me a dictator, you know – and bossy and bad-tempered."

Darrell stared at her in horror. "Moira – you wouldn't think *I* did it, would you? Or Sally? Or Alicia – or . . . "

Moira shrugged her shoulders and turned away. Darrell stared after her in dismay. She turned to Sally.

"We *must* find out who it is. We can't have

130

Moira suspecting every one of us! Gosh, what will the rehearsals be like if this kind of thing goes on?"

The fourth note didn't get to the person it was intended for. It was certainly slipped, unfolded, into a book on Moira's desk – but the book happened to be one that Miss Potts had lent Moira about play production. And having finished with it, Moira handed it back to Miss Potts without discovering the anonymous note inside.

So it was Miss Potts who found it. It slipped out on to the floor in the room she shared with Mam'zelle. She picked it up and read it.

Are you worrying about these notes? There are plenty more to come! I've got quite a few more names to call you, and adjectives that will suit you. How about the Demon Queen? You look like a demon sometimes. A domineering, bossy, scowling, glowering one, too. At least, that's how you appear to

ME

Miss Potts was amazed at this note. She read it over again. Who was it meant for? She turned it over and saw a name printed on the back. MOIRA!

"Moira!" she said. "So somebody slipped it into the book I lent her. An anonymous note – and a particularly spiteful one. Who in the world is low enough to think out things like these?"

She examined the writing. It gave her no clue, because all the letters were in capitals, very carefully done. Miss Potts frowned as she stood there. Like all decent people she thought that anonymous letter-writers were either mad or cowardly. They didn't dare to say what they thought openly – they had to do it secretly and loathsomely.

She sent for Moira. Moira told her about the other

132

notes. "Have you any idea at all who sent these?" asked Miss Potts.

Moira hesitated. "Yes. But I'm not sure about it, so I can't say."

"Go and get Darrell, and Sally, too," said Miss Potts, thinking she could probably get more out of them. "This has got to be stopped. Once a person of this sort gets away with a thing like this there's no knowing what they'll do next."

Sally and Darrell came. They read the note. Darrell looked sick. "Horrible," she said.

"Who has written them?" demanded Miss Potts.

All three girls looked away. "Well?" said Miss Potts, impatiently. "This is not a thing to be backward about, is it? Don't you agree that it must be stopped?"

"Oh *yes*," said Darrell.

"Well then – if you have any idea who has written them, tell me," said Miss Potts. "I can then go and tackle them at once."

"Well – you see – it might be one of quite a number of people," said Darrell.

"A *number* of people?" said Miss Potts, disbelievingly. "Are you trying to tell me that there are a *number* of people who hate Moira enough to write her notes like this?"

There was a silence. Miss Potts clicked in exasperation. "Has Moira so many enemies? And why? I have had no complaints of her as head girl. Why do you think so many people hate Moira?"

This was very awkward and most embarrassing. Darrell and Sally didn't know what in the world to say. Moira came to their rescue. She was pale, and looked strained.

"*I'll* tell who it might be, Miss Potts!" she said. "It might be Gwen. It might be Maureen. It might even be Alicia."

"No!" said both Sally and Darrell together.

Moira went on. "It might be Catherine. It might be – it might be Bridget."

"*Bridget* – do you mean your sister in the fourth?" asked Miss Potts, amazed.

Moira nodded, looking miserable. She wouldn't look at Sally or Darrell. Miss Potts turned to them. "What do you think of all this?" she demanded.

"Well – it *could* be any of those except Alicia," said Darrell. "Alicia *does* feel angry with Moira because of something that happened at a rehearsal – but Alicia's not underhanded. If she wanted to tell Moira all those things she'd say them out loud, probably in front of everyone, too! It's certainly not Alicia."

"I agree with you," said Miss Potts. "We can certainly rule out Alicia. That still leaves four people that Moira thinks detest her enough to write these notes. Moira – it's rather dreadful to feel you have four people around you that might regard you with such bitter feelings, isn't it? What *can* you have been doing to arouse them?"

Moira said nothing. She knew perfectly well why all four had cause to hate her. She had sneered at Gwen and Maureen unmercifully, and had humiliated them too, on the stage at last week's rehearsal. She had called Catherine a doormat and sneered too at her, for her annoying self-sacrificing ways, and had shoved her to one side, in spite of all the hundreds of things Catherine had done for her.

As for Bridget – well, there never had been any love lost between the sisters. Bridget hated her, she was sure of it. And hadn't Bridget threatened her not so long ago? What had she said, "I warn you, Moira, you'll be sorry for this. I *warn* you!"

Well – it might be Catherine, it might be Gwen or Maureen, and it might be Bridget. It probably *wasn't*

Alicia – because these letters came from a coward, and nobody could call Alicia that!

Who *did* write those beastly letters? And how could they ever find out?

Things Happen

All sorts of things happened that week. At the next rehearsal there was another flare-up between Alicia and Moira – a really bad one that ended in Alicia resigning from the show! Betty promptly resigned, too, as co-producer.

It was a terrible blow to Sally and Darrell. "We *can't* do without you, Alicia," wailed Darrell. "We'll never, never get a demon king like you – and all your wonderful juggling and conjuring and leaping about, too. You'll ruin the whole thing if you resign."

"*If* I resign! I *have* resigned!" said Alicia, looking calm and unruffled, but inwardly seething with anger, disappointment and misery at seeing Darrell so upset. "I'm sorry it affects you too – but I'm not working with Moira any more. And nothing in the world will make me go back into the pantomime now – no, not even if Moira herself resigned and came and apologized."

Darrell knew that Moira would never do *that*. She was as unbending as Alicia was obstinate.

"Talk about the immovable meeting the irresistible!" she groaned. "Oh, Alicia – for *my* sake, withdraw your resignation. Why, it's only three weeks now till the pantomime is presented. I can't rewrite it, and cut out your parts – you come in so often."

"Darrell, I'm honestly sorry," said Alicia, looking

harassed now. "But you know I never go back on my word. It's my pride now that's in the way. Nothing in the world would make me knuckle under to Moira – and that's what I should be doing if I withdrew my resignation."

Darrell stared hopelessly at Alicia. Defiant, obstinate, strong-willed Alicia – nobody could do anything with her once she had made up her mind. She turned away, amazed and furious to find sudden tears in her eyes. But she was so bitterly disappointed. Her lovely pantomime – and such a wonderful demon king – and all that juggling and conjuring out of it now. No one but Alicia could do that.

Sally went with Darrell, trying to comfort her. She, too, was bitterly disappointed, and sighed when she thought of all the rewriting there would be to do – and another demon king to find and train in such a short time. But Darrell felt it most. It was her first big job, the first time she had tried her hand at writing something worthwhile – and now it was spoilt.

Moira was obstinate too. She would not talk about the matter at all. Nor would she resign. "All I can say is, I'm sorry it's happened, but it was Alicia who blew up and resigned, not me," she said. And not one word more would she say about it.

It was Mam'zelle who created the next excitement. She sat down at her desk in Miss Potts' room one day, and announced her intention of turning it out.

"About time, too," said Miss Potts, dryly. "You'll probably find the year before last's exam papers there, I should think. I never saw such a collection of rubbish in anyone's desk in my life."

"Ha, Miss Potts! You wish to be funny?" said Mam'zelle, huffily.

"No," said Miss Potts. "Merely truthful."

Mam'zelle snorted, and took hold of about a hundred loose papers in her desk. She lifted them out and they immediately fell apart and slithered all over the floor. One booklet floated to Miss Potts' feet. She looked at it with interest, for there was a very brightly coloured picture on the cover, showing a conjurer doing tricks. "New tricks. Old tricks. Tricks to play on your enemies. Tricks to play on your friends," she read out loud. She glanced at Mam'zelle in astonishment. "Since when did you think of taking up tricks to play?" she inquired.

"I do not think of it," said Mam'zelle, depositing another hundred papers on the floor. "*Tiens!* Here is the programme of the play the third-formers gave six years ago!"

"What did I tell you?" said Miss Potts. "You'll probably find the Speeches made at the Opening of the First Term at Malory Towers if you look a little further into your desk."

"Do not tizz me," said Mam'zelle. "I do not like being tizzed."

"I'm not teasing," said Miss Potts. "I'm quite serious. I say – *where* did you get these trick and conjuring lists from? Look at this one – I'm sure it's got in it all the tricks that Alicia and Betty ever played on you!"

Mam'zelle took the booklets. She was soon completely absorbed in them. She chuckled. She laughed. She said "*Tiens!*" and "Oh, *là là!*" a dozen times. Miss Potts went on with her work. She was used to Mam'zelle's little ways.

Mam'zelle had never read anything so enthralling in all her life as these booklets that described tricks of all sorts and kinds. She was completely lost in them. She read of machines that could apparently saw people's fingers in half without hurting them – cigarettes with glowing ends that were not really alight – ink spots and jam-clots that could be placed on tablecloths to deceive annoyed mothers or teachers into thinking they were real.

The booklets blandly described these and a hundred others. Mam'zelle was absolutely fascinated. She came to one trick that made her laugh out loud. "Ah, now listen, Miss Potts," she began.

"*No*, Mam'zelle," said Miss Potts, sternly. "I've twenty-three *disgrace*ful maths papers to mark that the first form have had the nerve to give in today – and I do NOT want to listen to your recital of childish tricks."

Mam'zelle sighed and went back to the booklets. She read over again the thing that had so intrigued her. There were two photographs with the description of the trick. One showed a smiling man with ordinary teeth – the other showed the same man – with trick teeth. He looked horrible.

Mam'zelle read the description over again. "These trick teeth are cleverly made of celluloid, and are shaped to fit neatly over the wearer's own teeth – but project forwards and downwards, and so alter the expression of the wearer's face considerably as soon as he smiles, giving a really terrifying and exceedingly strange appearance."

Mam'zelle studied the photographs. She tried to imagine herself wearing teeth like that – and suddenly flashing them at the girls with a smile. Ha! They had dared her to do a trick on them! Mam'zelle had a very very good mind to write for this teeth trick. Perhaps she would wear them at a lacrosse match out in the field – or maybe take the girls for a walk, and keep showing her trick teeth.

Mam'zelle shook with laughter. Ha ha – so many "treeks" had those bad girls played on her, it was time their poor old Mam'zelle played a "treek" on them too.

How they would be astonished! How they would stare. How they would laugh afterwards.

Mam'zelle scuffled about among her untidy papers and found her writing-pad. In her slanting French handwriting she wrote for the "teeth trick" and sent a cheque with the letter. She was delighted. She would not tell even Miss Potts.

"No. I will not tell her. I will suddenly smile at her – like this," said Mam'zelle to herself – and did a sudden fierce grin – "and I shall look so strange that she will start back in fright at my horrible teeth."

Mam'zelle finished the letter and then casually looked through the other trick booklets before throwing them away. And it was then she came across the note. It was written in capitals, very carefully. It was not a nice note. It was headed:

TO FELICITY

You think you're so good at games, don't you? Well, it's only because Darrell favours you that you're ever put into any teams. Everyone knows that!

It was not signed at all. "Here is a nasty little note," said Mam'zelle in disgust, and tossed it to Miss Potts. Miss Potts recognized the printed letters at once – they were exactly the same as those on the anonymous letters sent to Moira.

"Where did you get this?" she asked, sharply.

"I found it in this trick booklet," said Mam'zelle, startled.

"Whose is the booklet? Where did you get it?" demanded Miss Potts.

"I took it from that bad little June's desk," said Mam'zelle.

"Very interesting," said Miss Potts. She got up and went to the door. She sent a girl to find Moira, Sally and Darrell. They came, looking surprised.

"I think I've found the writer of those notes," said Miss Potts. "But before I tackle her I want to know if she's any reason to dislike you, Moira. It's June, in the first form."

"*June!*" exclaimed everyone, amazed.

Moira looked at Miss Potts. "Yes – I suppose she'd think she had cause to dislike me," she said. "I ticked her off because she was cheeky about not being put into the Wellsbrough match. Told her she had no team spirit. I also made her apologize to me for daring to say in front of me that Darrell had put Felicity into the match out of favouritism, because she was her sister."

Miss Potts nodded. "Thank you. It *is* June then, I'm afraid. I'll see her now. Send her to me, will you. I'm rather afraid this is a matter for Miss Grayling. We are not pleased with June and it wouldn't take much to have her sent away from here. This is a particularly loathsome act of hers – to send out anonymous letters."

June came, looking defiant but scared. She had not been told why she was wanted.

"June, I have called you here on a very very serious matter," said Miss Potts. "I find that you have been writing detestable anonymous letters. Don't attempt to deny it. You will only make things worse. Your only hope is to confess honestly. Why did you do it?"

June had no idea how Miss Potts knew all this. She went white, but still looked bold. "I suppose you mean the ones to Moira?" she said. "Yes, I did write them – and she deserved them. Everyone hates her."

"That's beside the point," said Miss Potts. "The point we have to keep to is that there is a girl in this school, a girl in the first form, who is guilty of something for which in later years she could be sent to prison – a thing that as a rule rarely begins until a girl is much much older than you, because it is only depraved and cowardly characters who attempt this underhand, stab-in-the-back kind of thing."

She paused. Her eyes bored like gimlets into the petrified June.

"We call this kind of thing 'poison-pen' writing, when the writers are grown up," she went on, "and they are held in universal loathing and hatred, considered the lowest of the low. Did you know that?"

"No," gasped June.

"I would not talk to you in this serious manner if there were not also other things I dislike very much in you," said Miss Potts, still in the same hard, driving voice. "Your disobedience, your defiance, your aggressiveness, your total lack of respect for anyone. You may think it is admirable and brave and grand. It isn't. It is the sign of a strong character gone wrong – and on top of all that you have shown yourself a coward – because only a coward ever writes anonymous letters."

June's knees were shaking. Miss Potts saw them but she took no notice. If ever anyone wanted a good shaking up it was June.

"This matter must go to Miss Grayling," she said. "Come with me now. You may be interested to know that it was because Mam'zelle found this note – to Felicity – that I discovered who was the writer of the other letters."

June took a quick glance at the note to Felicity. "I didn't give it to her," she said. "I meant to – and then I didn't. I must have left it somewhere in a book."

"Our sins always find us out," said Miss Potts, solemnly. "Always. Now, come with me."

"Miss Potts – shall I be – be – expelled?" asked June – a June no longer bold and brazen, but a June as deflated as when her balloons had been suddenly pricked that day in class.

"That rests with Miss Grayling," said Miss Potts, and she got up. "Come."

The news went round the fifth form rapidly. "The letters were written by June – the little beast!"

"She's gone to see Miss Grayling. I bet she'll be expelled. She's no good, anyway."

Alicia listened in horror. Her own cousin! She disliked June as much as anybody else – but this was her own cousin in terrible trouble and disgrace. She was very distressed.

"It's a disgrace for our whole family," she thought. "And what *will* June's people say? They'll never get over it if she's expelled. They'll think I ought to have kept an eye on June more – and perhaps I should. But she really is such a little beast!"

Felicity came tearing up to the fifth-form common room that evening. She was in tears. "Darrell!" she said, hardly waiting to knock. "Oh, Darrell – June's going to be expelled. She is really. Miss Grayling told her so. Oh, *Darrell* – I don't like her – but I can't bear her to be expelled. Surely she's not as bad as all that."

Everyone in the fifth-form common room sat up with a jerk at this news. Expelled! It was ages since anyone had been sent in disgrace from Malory Towers. And a first-former, too. Alicia sat silent, biting her lips. Her own cousin. How terrible.

Poor Felicity began to sob. "June's got to go tomorrow. Miss Grayling is telephoning her parents tonight. She's packing now, this minute. She's terribly, terribly upset. She keeps saying she's not a coward, and she didn't *know* it was so awful, she keeps on and on . . . Darrell, can't you do something? Suppose it was *me*, Darrell? Wouldn't you do something?"

The fifth form were aghast at all this. They pictured

June packing, bewildered and frightened. Miss Grayling must have had very bad reports of her to make her go to this length. She must have thought there was no good in June at all not to give her one more chance.

"Darrell! Sally! Alicia! Can't you go and ask Miss Grayling to give her a chance?" cried Felicity, a big tear running down her nose and falling on to the carpet. "I tell you, she's *awfully* upset."

Moira had been listening with the others. So it *was* June! She looked round at Gwen, Maureen and Catherine, three of the girls she had suspected. It was a load off her heart that it wasn't any of them. It was an even greater relief that it wasn't Bridget, her sister.

But suppose it had been? It would have been Bridget who was packing then – Bridget who would have been so "awfully upset". It would have been her own parents who would be so sad and miserable because a child of theirs had been expelled.

Moira got up. "*I'll* go and see Miss Grayling," she said. "I won't let her expel June. I'll ask her to give her another chance. After all – I've been pretty awful myself this term – and it's not to be wondered at if a mere first-former hated me – and descended to writing those letters. There was quite a lot of truth in them! June deserves to be punished – but not so badly as that."

She went out of the room, leaving behind a deep silence. Felicity ran with her, and actually took her hand! Moira squeezed it. "Oh, Moira – people say you're hard and unkind – but you're not, you're not!" said little Felicity. "You're kind and generous and good, and I shall tell every single person in the first form so!"

Nobody ever knew what happened between Miss Grayling, Moira and June, for not one of the three ever said. But the result was that June was sent to unpack her things again, very subdued and thankful, and that Moira came back to find a common room full of admiration and goodwill towards her.

"It's all right," said Moira, smiling round a little nervously. "June's let off. She's unpacking again. She won't forget this lesson in a hurry."

Alicia spoke in a rather shaky voice. "Thanks most awfully, Moira. You've been most frightfully decent over this. I can't ever repay you – it means an awful lot to me to know that my cousin won't be expelled. I – er – I – want to apologize for resigning from the pantomime. If – if you'll let me withdraw my resignation, I'd like to."

This was a very difficult thing for Alicia to do – Alicia who had said that nothing in the world would make her withdraw her resignation or apologize! Well, something *had* made her – and she was decent enough and brave enough not to shirk the awkwardness and difficulty but to say it all straight out in public.

Everyone went suddenly mad. Darrell gave a squeal of delight and rushed to Alicia. Sally thumped her on the back. Mavis sang loudly. Irene went to the piano and played a triumphant march from the pantomime. Bill and Clarissa galloped round the room as if they were on horseback, and little Mary-Lou thumped on the top of the table. Moira laughed suddenly.

What had happened to all the spite and malice and beastliness? What had happened to the squabbles and quarrels and worries? They were gone in an instant, blown to smithereens by Moira's instinctive, generous-hearted action in going to save June.

"Everything's right again," sang Mavis, and Mary-Lou thumped the table in time. "Everything's right, everything's right – HURRAY!"

Certainly everything was much better now. Alicia went to see June and addressed a good many sound and sensible words to that much chastened and subdued first-former. It would be a long time before June forgot them, if she ever did. She didn't think she ever would.

Moira was basking in a new-found admiration and liking that made her much more amenable to the others's suggestions, and rehearsals became a pleasure. Even the sulky Bridget came smiling into the fifth-form common room to say she was glad Moira had saved June. "It makes me feel you might do the same for *me*, Moira!" she said.

"Well – I would," said Moira, shortly, and Bridget went out, pleased.

Mam'zelle had been very shocked and upset about everything. "But it is terrible! How could June do such a thing? And Moira – *Moira*, that hard Moira to go and save her like that! Miss Potts, never would I have thought that girl had a generous action in her! Miss Potts – it shocks me that I know so little of my girls!"

"Oh, you'll get over the shock," said Miss Potts, cheerfully. "And you'll have plenty more. Well, well – the girls have cheered up a lot – the fifth-formers, I mean. They really were a worried, miserable, quarrelsome crew last week! I was seriously thinking of playing a trick on them to cheer them up!"

Mam'zelle looked at Miss Potts. In her desk were the trick teeth which had arrived that morning. Miss

Potts must not play a trick – if a trick was to be played, she, Mam'zelle, would play it. Ah yes – to cheer up the poor girls! That would be a kind act to do.

There was a house match that afternoon – North Tower girls against West Tower. Mam'zelle decided she would appear as a spectator at the match – with her teeth!

Ah, those teeth! Mam'zelle had tried them on. They might have been made for her! They fitted over her own teeth, but were longer, and projected slightly forward. They were not noticeable at all, of course, when she had her mouth shut – but when she smiled – ah, how sinister she looked, how strange, how fierce!

Mam'zelle had shocked even herself when she had put in the extraordinary teeth and smiled at herself in the glass. "*Tiens!*" she said, and clutched her dressing-table. "I am a monster! I am truly terrible with these teeth . . . "

That afternoon she put them in carefully over her others and went downstairs to the playing-fields, wrapping herself up warmly in coat, scarf and turban. Darrell saw her first, and made room for her on the form she was on.

"Thank you," said Mam'zelle, and smiled at Darrell. Darrell got a tremendous shock. Mam'zelle had suddenly looked altogether different – quite terrifying. Darrell stared at her – but Mam'zelle had quickly shut her mouth.

The next one to get the Smile was little Felicity who came up with Susan. Mam'zelle smiled at her.

"Oh!" said Felicity in sudden horror, and Susan stared. Mam'zelle shut her mouth. A desire to laugh was gradually working up inside her. No, no – she must not laugh. Laughing spoilt tricks.

She did not smile for some time, trying to conquer

146

her urge to laugh. Miss Linnie, the sewing mistress, passed by and nodded at Mam'zelle. Mam'zelle could not resist showing her the teeth. She smiled.

Miss Linnie looked amazed and horrified. She walked on quickly. "Was that *really* Mam'zelle?" she wondered. "No, it must have been someone else. What awful teeth!"

Mam'zelle felt that she must get up and walk about. It was too cold to sit – and besides she so badly wanted to laugh again. Ah, now she understood why the girls laughed so much and so helplessly when they played their mischievous tricks on her.

She walked along the field, and met Bill and Clarissa. They smiled at her and she smiled back. Bill stood still, thunderstruck. Clarissa hadn't really noticed.

"Clarissa!" said Bill, when Mam'zelle had gone. "What's the matter with Mam'zelle this afternoon? She looks *horrible!*"

"Horrible? How?" asked Clarissa in great surprise.

"Well, her *teeth*! Didn't you see her teeth?" asked Bill. "They seem to have changed or something. Simply awful teeth she had – long and sticking-out."

Clarissa was astonished. "Let's walk back and smile at her again," she said. So back they went. But Mam'zelle saw their inquisitive looks, and was struggling against a fit of laughter. She would not open her mouth to smile.

Matron came up. "Oh, Mam'zelle – do you know where Gwen is? She's darned her navy gym pants with grey wool again. I want her indoors this afternoon!"

Mam'zelle could not resist smiling at Matron. Matron stared as if she couldn't believe her eyes. Mam'zelle shut her mouth. Matron backed away a little, looking rather alarmed.

"Gwen's over there," said Mam'zelle, her extra teeth

making her words sound rather thick. Matron looked even more alarmed at the thick voice and disappeard in a hurry. Mam'zelle saw her address a few words to Miss Potts. Miss Potts looked round for Mam'zelle.

"Aha!" thought Mam'zelle. "Matron has told her I look terrible! Soon Miss Potts will come to look at my Smile. I shall laugh. I know I shall. I shall laugh without stopping soon."

Miss Potts came up, eyeing Mam'zelle carefully. She got a quick glimpse of the famous teeth. Then Mam'zelle clamped her mouth shut. She would explode if she didn't keep her mouth shut! She pulled her scarf across her face, trying to hide her desire to laugh.

"Do you feel the cold today, Mam'zelle?" asked Miss Potts anxiously. "You – er – you haven't got toothache, have you?"

A peculiar wild sound came from Mam'zelle. It startled Miss Potts considerably. But actually it was only Mam'zelle trying to stifle a squeal of laughter. She rushed away hurriedly. Miss Potts stared after her uncomfortably. What *was* up with Mam'zelle?

Mam'zelle strolled down the field by herself, trying to recover. She gave a few loud gulps that made two second-formers wonder if she was going to be ill.

Poor Mam'zelle felt she couldn't flash her teeth at anyone for a long time, for if she did she would explode like Irene. She decided to go in. She turned her steps towards the school – and then, to her utter horror, she saw Miss Grayling, the headmistress, bearing down on her with two parents! Mam'zelle gave an anguished look and hurried on as fast as she could.

"Oh – there's Mam'zelle," said Miss Grayling's pleasant voice. "Mam'zelle, will you meet Mrs Jennings and Mrs Petton?"

Mam'zelle was forced to go to them. She lost all

desire for laughter at once. The trick teeth suddenly stopped being funny, and became monstrosities to be got rid of at once. But how? She couldn't spit them into her handkerchief with people just about to shake hands with her.

Mrs Jennings held out her hand. "I've heard so much about you, Mam'zelle Dupont," she said, "and what tricks the naughty girls play on you, too!"

Mam'zelle tried to smile without opening her mouth at all, and the effect was rather peculiar – a sort of suppressed snarl. Mrs Jennings looked surprised. Mam'zelle tried to make up for her lack of smile by shaking Mrs Jennings' hand very vigorously indeed.

She did the same with Mrs Petton, who turned out to be a talkative mother who wanted to know *exactly* how her daughter Teresa was getting on in French. She smiled gaily at Mam'zelle while she talked, and Mam'zelle found it agony not to smile back. She had to produce the suppressed snarl again, smiling with her mouth shut and her lips firmly over her teeth.

Miss Grayling was startled by this peculiar smile. She examined Mam'zelle closely. Mam'zelle's voice was not quite as usual either – it sounded thick. "As if her mouth is too full of teeth," thought Miss Grayling, little knowing that she had hit on the exact truth.

At last the mothers went. Mam'zelle shook hands with them most vigorously once more, and was so relieved at parting from them that she forgot herself and gave them a broad smile.

They got a full view of the terrible teeth, Miss Grayling, too. The head stared in the utmost horror – *what* had happened to Mam'zelle's teeth? Had she had her old ones out – were these a new, false set? But how TERRIBLE they were! They made her look like the wolf in the tale of Red Riding Hood.

The two mothers turned their heads away quickly

at the sight of the teeth. They hurried off with Miss Grayling who hardly heard what they said, she was so concerned about Mam'zelle's teeth. She determined to send for Mam'zelle that evening and ask her about them. Really – she couldn't allow any of her staff to go about with teeth like that! They were monstrous, hideous!

Mam'zelle was so thankful to see the last of the mothers that she hurried straight into a little company of fifth-formers going back to the school, some to do their piano practice and some to have a lesson in elocution.

"Hallo, Mam'zelle!" said Mavis. "Are you coming back to school?"

Mam'zelle smiled. The fifth-formers got a dreadful shock. They stared in silent horror. The teeth had slipped a little, and now looked rather like fangs. They gave Mam'zelle a most sinister, big-bad-wolf look. Mam'zelle saw their alarm and astonishment. Laughter surged back into her. She felt it swelling up and up. She gasped. She gulped. She roared.

She sank on to a bench and cried with helpless laughter. She remembered Matron's face – and Miss Grayling's – and the faces of the two mothers. The more she thought of them the more helplessly she laughed. The girls stood round, more alarmed than ever. What *was* the matter with Mam'zelle? What was this enormous joke?

Mam'zelle's teeth slipped out altogether, fell on to her lap, and then to the ground. The girls stared at them in the utmost amazement, and then looked at Mam'zelle. She now looked completely normal, with just her own small teeth showing in her laughing face. She laughed on and on when she saw her trick teeth lying there before her.

"It is a treek," she squeaked at last, wiping her eyes

with her handkerchief. "Did you not give me a dare? Did you not tell me to do a treek on you? I have done one with the teeth. They are treek teeth. Oh, *là là* – I must laugh again. Oh my sides, oh my back!"

She swayed to and fro, laughing. The girls began to laugh, too. Mam'zelle Rougier came up, astonished to see the other French mistress laughing so much.

"What is the matter?" she asked, without a smile on her face.

Irene did one of her explosions. She pointed to the teeth on the ground. "Mam'zelle wore them – for a trick – and they've fallen out and given the game away!"

She went off into squeals of laughter again, and the others girls joined in. Mam'zelle Rougier looked cold and disapproving.

"I see no joke," she said. "It is not funny, teeth on the grass. It is time to see the dentist when that happens."

She walked off, and her speech and disapproving face sent everyone into fits of laughter again. It was altogether a most successful afternoon for Mam'zelle, and the "treek" story flew all through the school immediately.

Mam'zelle suddenly found herself extremely popular, except with the staff. "A little *undignified*, don't you think?" said Miss Williams.

"Not a thing to do *too* often, Mam'zelle," said Miss Potts, making up her mind to remove the trick booklets from Mam'zelle's desk at the first opportunity.

"Glad you've lost those frightful teeth," said Matron, bluntly. "Don't do that again without warning me, Mam'zelle. I got the shock of my life."

But the girls loved Mam'zelle for her "treek", and every class in the school, from top to bottom, worked twice as hard (or so Mam'zelle declared) after she had played her truly astonishing "treek"!

A Grand Show

The end of the term was coming near. The pantomime was almost ready. Everything had gone smoothly since the Big Row, as it was called.

Moira had softened down a lot, pleased by the unstinted admiration of the girls for her act in going down to the head to speak for June. Alicia was back as demon king, as good as ever, complete with eerie chant. Betty was back as co-producer. Everyone knew her part perfectly.

Belinda's scenery was almost finished. She had produced all kinds of wonderful effects, helped by the properties "Pop" had out in the barn – relics of other plays and pantomimes. She painted fast and furiously, and Pop had helped to evolve a magnificent coach which they had somehow managed to adorn with gilt paint.

"It looks marvellous," said Clarissa, in awe. "I suppose Merrylegs couldn't pull it, Belinda? He'd be awfully good, I know."

"I daresay – but if you think I'm going to have Thunder and Merrylegs galloping about madly all over my precious stage, you can think again," said Belinda, adding a final touch of gilt to a wheel.

All the actors knew the songs, both words and music. The costumes were ready. Janet had done well, and everyone had a costume that fitted and suited the wearer perfectly. Cinderella looked enchanting in her ballgown – a dress whose full skirt floated out mistily, glittering with hundreds of sequins patiently sewn on by the first-formers in their sewing class.

The whole school was interested in the pantomime because so many of them had either helped to paint the scenery or make the props or sew the costumes. They were all looking forward tremendously to the show the next week.

Gwen and Maureen looked enviously at Mary-Lou in her ballgown. How they wished they could wear a frock like that. How beautiful they would look!

Catherine gazed at little Mary-Lou, too. She had become very fond of her. Mary-Lou was gentle and timid and always grateful for anything that Catherine did for her. She didn't call her a doormat or laugh at her self-sacrificing ways. She didn't even call her Saint Catherine as the others did.

Catherine had stopped being a doormat for the form. She had felt angry and sore about it. But she somehow couldn't stop waiting on people – and Mary-Lou didn't mind! So she fussed over her, and altered her frock, and praised her, and heard her words; and altogether she made life very easy for Mary-Lou, who was really very nervous about taking the principal part in the show.

Now the days were spinning away fast – Friday, Saturday, Sunday, Monday – two more days left, one more day . . .

"And now it's THE DAY!" cried Darrell the next morning, rushing to the window. "And it's a heavenly day, so all the parents will get down without any bother. Gosh, I feel so excited I don't know what I'm doing."

"Well, you certainly don't know the difference between my sponge and yours," said Sally, taking her own sponge away from the excited Darrell. "Come on

– get dressed, idiot. We've got a lot to do today!"

The parents arrived at tea time. Tea was at four. The pantomime was due to begin at half past five, and went on till half past seven. Then there came a Grand Supper, and after that the parents went – some to their homes, if they were within driving distance, some to hotels.

The tea was grand and the first and second-formers scurried about with plates and dishes, helping themselves to the meringues and éclairs whenever they could. The fifth-formers slipped away to dress at half past four. Darrell peeped at the stage.

How big it looked – how grand! It was already set for the first scene, with a great fireplace for Cinderella to sit by. Darrell felt solemn. She had written this pantomime. If it was a failure she would never never write anything again – and you never knew – it might be a terrible flop.

Sally came up. She saw Darrell's solemn face and smiled. "It's going to be a terrific success," she said. "You just see! And you'll deserve it, Darrell – you really have worked hard."

"So have you," said Darrell, loyally – but Sally knew that the creative part had all been Darrell's. The words and the songs had all come out of Darrell's own imagination. Sally hadn't much imagination – she was sensible and sturdy and stolid. She admired Darrell for her quick creativeness without envying her.

The school orchestra were in their places, tuning up. They had learnt all Irene's music, and she was going to conduct them. She looked flushed and pleased.

"Are you nervous?" asked Belinda.

"Yes. *Now* I am. But at the very first stroke of my baton, at the very first note of the music, I'll forget to be nervous. I just won't be there. I'll be the music," said Irene. Belinda understood this remarkable statement very well, and nodded gravely.

The actors were all dressed in their costumes. Mary-Lou had on her ragged Cinderella frock and looked frightened. "But it doesn't matter you looking pensive and scared," Moira told her. "You're just right like that – Cinderella to the life!"

Alicia looked simply magnificent. She was dressed in a tight-fitting glowing red costume that showed off her slim figure perfectly. It was glittering with bright sequins. Her eyes glittered, too. She wore a pointed hood and looked "positively *wicked*", Betty said.

"And don't you drop any of your juggling rings, and discover your rabbit isn't in your hat after all, or something," she said to Alicia. But Alicia knew she wouldn't. Alicia wasn't nervous – she was cocksure and confident and brilliant-eyed, and leapt about as if she had springs in her heels.

"Shhhhhhh!" said somebody. "The orchestra's beginning. The audience are all coming in. Shhhhh!"

The orchestra played a lively rousing tune. Lovely! Darrell peeped through the curtains and saw Irene standing up, conducting vigorously. What did it feel like to conduct your own music? Just as good as it would feel to see your own play acted, no doubt. She shivered in excitement.

A bell rang behind stage. The curtains were about to swing open. The chorus got ready to go in. The pantomime had begun!

When the chorus danced off the stage, Mary-Lou was left by the fire as Cinderella. She sang – and her small sweet voice caught Irene's lilting melodies, making everyone listen intently.

The Baron came on – Bill, stamping around in riding boots, roaring here and roaring there.

"It's BILL!" shouted the delighted school and

clapped so much that they held up the pantomime for a bit. The two Ugly Sisters brought down the house too. They were perfectly hideous, perfectly idiotic and perfectly wonderful. And how they enjoyed themselves! Gwen even found herself wishing she might have been one of them! Ugly or not, it must be wonderful to have a comic part like that. But Gwen was only a servant in the chorus, unseen and almost unheard!

Mrs Lacy hardly caught sight of her at all. But for once in a way she didn't mind – she was so enraptured with the pantomime.

Then the Prince came – tall, slender Mavis, looking shy and nervous until she had to sing – and then what a marvel! Her voice broke on the startled audience like a miracle, and there was not a single sound to be heard while she sang.

Mothers found their eyes full of tears. What a wonderful voice! What a good thing it had come back to Mavis. Why, one day she would be a great opera singer, perhaps the greatest that ever lived. Mavis sang on and on like a bird, her voice pure and true, and Irene exulted in the tunes she had written so well for her.

There was such a storm of clapping that again the pantomime was held up. "Encore!" shouted everyone. "Encore! ENCORE!"

Darrell was trembling with excitement and joy. It was a success. It WAS a success. In fact, it looked like being a SUPER success. She could hardly keep still.

Alicia was excellent. She leapt on magnificently, with her eerie chant. "Ooooooh!" said the lower school, deliciously thrilled. "The demon king. It's Alicia!"

Without a single mistake Alicia juggled and tumbled, did cartwheels and conjured as if she had been doing nothing else all her life. Fathers turned to one another and exclaimed in astonished admiration.

"She's good enough to be on the London stage. How on earth did she do *that* trick?"

So the show went on, and everyone clapped and cheered madly at the end of the first act. The actors rushed to Moira and Darrell when the curtain came down at the end of the act.

"Are we doing all right? I nearly forgot my lines! Isn't the audience grand? Oh, Darrell, aren't you *proud*? Moira, we're doing fine, aren't we? Aren't we?"

The second act was performed. Now the audience had time to appreciate the lovely costumes and marvel at them. They marvelled at the scenery, too – and applauded the gilt coach frantically, especially the lower school, some of whom had helped to paint it.

And then at last the end came. The final chorus was sung, the last bow made. The curtain swung back once – twice – three – four times. The audience rose to its feet, cheering and shouting and stamping. It was the biggest success Malory Towers had ever had.

The audience sat down. A call came that grew more and more insistent.

"Author! *Author!* AUTHOR!"

Someone gave Darrell a push. "Go on, silly. They're calling for you. You're the author! You wrote it all!"

Blindly Darrell stepped out in front of the curtain. She saw Felicity's excited face somewhere. She searched for her father and mother. There they were – clapping wildly. Mrs Rivers found tears running down her face. Darrell! Her Darrell! How wonderful it was to have a child you could be proud of! Well done, Darrell, well done!

"Speech!" came a call. "Speech! Speeeeeech!"

"Say something, ass!" said Irene, from the orchestra. There was suddenly silence. Darrell hesitated. What should she say? "Thank you," she said, at last. "We – we did love doing it. I couldn't have done it by myself, of course. There was Irene, who wrote all the lovely music. Come up here, Irene!"

Irene came up beside her and bowed. She was clapped and cheered.

"And there was Belinda who designed everything," went on Darrell, and Belinda was pushed out from behind the curtain, beside her. "And Sally helped me all the time." Out came Sally, blushing.

"Moira and Betty were co-producers," said Darrell, warming up a little. "Here they are. Oh, and Janet did all the costumes!"

They appeared, beaming, and got a large share of claps and cheers.

"And Mavis ought to come, too, because she helped so much with the singing – and trained the chorus," said Darrell. Mavis sidled out shyly, and got a tremendous ovation.

"Oh – and I mustn't forget Pop!" said Darrell – and much to everyone's delight out came the handyman in waistcoat and green baize apron looking completely bemused and extremely proud. He bowed several times and then disappeared like a jack-in-the-box.

And then it was really all over. One last long clap, one last long shout – it was over.

"I wish I could hold this moment for ever and ever," thought Darrell, peeping through the curtains once again. "My first play – my first success! I don't want this moment to go!"

Hold it then, Darrell, while we slip away. It's your own great moment. There'll never be another quite like it!

Stories of Mystery and Adventure by Enid Blyton

in Armada

Mystery Series

Secrets Series

ARMADA

All these books are available at your local bookshop or newsagent, or can be ordered from the publisher. To order direct from the publishers just tick the title you want and fill in the form below:

Name _____

Address _____

_____

Send to: Collins Childrens Cash Sales
          PO Box 11
          Falmouth
          Cornwall
          TR10 9EN

Please enclose a cheque or postal order or debit my Visa/ Access –

Credit card no:

Expiry date:

Signature:

– to the value of the cover price plus:

UK: 60p for the first book, 25p for the second book, plus 15p per copy for each additional book ordered to a maximum charge of £1.90.

BFPO: 60p for the first book, 25p for the second book plus 15p per copy for the next 7 books, thereafter 9p per book.

Overseas and Eire: £1.25 for the first book, 75p for the second book. Thereafter 28p per book.

ARMADA